GIGI MAKE PARADOX

WHERE THE HELL IS TESLA? BOOK 3

ROB DIRCKS

GOLDFINCH PUBLISHING

Published by Goldfinch Publishing
An Imprint of SARK Industries, Inc.
www.goldfinchpublishing.com

Publisher's Note:
This is a work of fiction. Names, characters, places, and incidents either are the product of the author's imagination or are used fictitiously. Any resemblance to actual persons, living or dead, events, or locales is entirely coincidental. Use of Nikola Tesla as historical figure and character have been approved by William Terbo, grand nephew and last living relative of Tesla.

Library of Congress Cataloging-in-Publication Data
Rob Dircks, 1967-
Gigi Make Paradox (Where the Hell is Tesla? Book 3) / by Rob Dircks
p. cm.
ISBN 978-1733017916

NOTICE:

Posted by Fred Morris,
Regional Director, New York City
Federal Bureau of Investigation

First, thank you, reader, for joining us on two journeys and now this third. Your willing acceptance that these stories are fiction has helped us perpetuate our misinformation campai- wait, I wasn't supposed to say that. *Delete.* It's not deleting. *Delete.* What in the ever-loving hell? *Delete.* Kim, honey, can you come here and take a look at this? I'm dictating and it won't stop. Yes, of course I hit escape, I'm hitting all the keys. Yes, I agree, this damn computer has a mind of its own, and we should get a new one. Maybe this weekend. I think there was a Best Buy flyer in the mail yesterday. What am I working on? Oh, they asked me to write an intro to Chip's new book to make sure people continue to think it's all fake. Chip Collins. Yes, I like him too, very much. But sometimes he can be such a royal pain in the ass, you'd know what I'm talking about if you had to work with him. Okay, thanks for your help, honey, whatever, I'm sure the FBI will edit this part out, they've got professionals for this kind of stuff.

All right then, computer, start recording again:

Ahem. Second, in these pages, reader, you'll find a description of something called a *paradox*. I want to be perfectly clear: never has the entire city, state, country, or planet been in any existential jeopardy by an uncontrollable tear in the fabric of reality that would collapse all time and space. All references to a paradox and the threat it poses, leaving absolutely nothing but The Void, are purely fantasy written by the author, Clarence "Chip" Collins. In addition, contrary to the claims contained in this book, neither Mister Collins nor any of his family or friends have ever saved the multiverse, and I'm not saying there even is such a thing as a multiverse, but if there was one, they didn't save it. Again.

Finally, if on the night of February 29, 2020 you happened to see an orange glow emanating from the New Yorker Hotel in Manhattan, that was the, uh, window washers, yes, the window washers had a little, um, chemical accident. No one was harmed, of course, and the windows were subsequently cleaned, and like I said, the fate of Earth was never in peril, not even for one white-knuckle, bowel-exploding moment.

And so, for the third time, I invite you to enjoy Mister Collins' tales of astonishing and far-fetched events that could never, ever happen. Ever.

Yours truly,
Fred Morris
Regional Director, New York City
Federal Bureau of Investigation

1. PULL MY FINGER

"Hey Pete. Pull my finger."

He waves it away like it's on fire. "Dude. You're going to start the next book with a fart joke?"

"What book?"

"Oh. They didn't tell you?"

"Didn't tell me what? Who?"

"Dude, you have to start reading your emails. Seriously. You know, the ones marked *Urgent: FBI Official Business.*"

"I delete them as fast as I can. They didn't tell me *what*, dude?"

Pete pulls my finger and yes, I squeak out a Rip Van Winkle. I wanted it to be a stinker, he deserves it for springing whatever this book thing is on me in the middle of guys' night out, but it's a loud one. The loud ones never stink. Damn.

Wait, guys' night out. I should explain. "Guys' night out" is actually code for guys' night *in*. Lately it's been our only chance to hang out at all, me and Pete, with all the FBI shit, and the ITA, and we're all having jobs and being responsible, like we're actually grownups or something with families and careers. So every other Thursday, Julie and Meg–

Hold on. Have I told you Pete moved back to this dimension? Shit. I don't think so. I'm just assuming you know what the fuck is going on as usual. Okay, anyway Pete and Meg decided to move back to our dimension after the whole Blue Juice craziness (*Don't Touch the Blue Stuff! Where the Hell is Tesla? Book* 2, available at bookstores everywhere in case you need to catch up, although I won't see a dime in royalties because the FBI is such a bunch of tightwads), anyway they moved back so we could both be hipster New York City parents and take up the whole sidewalk with our tandem thousand-dollar Swiss baby strollers while the poor schmucks behind us drag their offspring around on wooden sleds like that kid on *Game of Thrones*. I'm kidding, don't get the wrong idea, we have the regular *pick-the-cheapest-one-and-let's-get-the-hell-out-of-here* strollers from BuyBuy Baby. Not that any stroller is cheap enough for me, I was like "it's four wheels and a bucket, how much can it cost? I could make one from stuff around the apartment for five bucks," but I think I've beaten the stroller thing to death already, so let's move on.

Anyway, every other Thursday, Julie and Meg get to hang up their mommy hats for a night and go out and paint the town whatever color vomit is after six strawberry mojitos, and me and Pete babysit our two angels.

Let me clarify again: by "babysit" I mean "play video games while Gigi and Hannah dress Bobo up in girl clothes and try to smear eye shadow on his fur," and by "angels" I mean "anarchist toddlers from the ninth circle of Hell."

Don't get me wrong. Underneath all the anarchy, little Gigi Collins and Hannah Turner are sweet little fluffs of cotton candy, spun from the silk of fairy spiders who live in the clouds. When they actually sleep – yes, it does happen sometimes – me and Pete'll sneak in and spy on them snoring their barely-audible little kid snores, and holding hands in the kiddy bed, and man, shit doesn't get any closer to heaven on Earth than that. It's so sweet once I even leaned my head on Pete's shoulder, like "awww, will you look at that," and he was like "What the fuck are you doing?" and I was like "Shhhh! They're sleeping," and he whisper-shouted back, "Don't even think about resting your head on my shoulder. Ever."

Anyway, we're sitting here now playing Madden, I'm actually kicking Pete's ass, God I love this game because it's like one of three things I can do better than him, and I'm thinking about this book thing, and then I notice the complete lack of sound coming from the kids in the bedroom. Hmm. It's a little too quiet in there. "Hey, dude. Would it be horrible if I asked Gigi to get me a beer?"

"Yes. That'll be the one thing she remembers when she grows up. Dad made me get beers for him. That's it. Her one memory of you. You want that to be her one horrible memory of you? Go to town."

I harrumph and pause the game and get myself a beer, wondering if these kids'll ever be old enough to do all the lawn mowing (not that we have lawns up here in our second-floor apartment), and garbage duty, and beer-fetching. Probably never. Whatever.

When I plop back down, I can't get Pete's comment out of my head. "You think she'll remember *anything* good? I mean, we do cool shit all the time with her."

"No. But don't take it personally. Humans are wired to remember negative experiences better, way back in the primitive parts of our brains, so we can recall where the lions mauled our cave-mate last time and avoid walking past their den next time. It's just survival, dude. Feel-good memories don't help you stay alive. It's called negative bias."

"What, did you take a class on caveman psychology back in college? I thought you were a finance major."

"Dude. That's just shit everyone knows. Especially philosophy majors. Did you not take one psychology class? Don't you remember Professor Crenshaw, how every class she'd remind us how we literally live better than kings from medieval times, but we'd still complain about the three-minute walk from her classroom back to the dorm? Which do you remember? Her talks or the walk?"

"The walk. I froze my ass off in the winter."

"Bingo. Negative bias."

"Whatever. You think I can start manually inserting good memories into her brain now, like *Inception*-style?"

"No."

I ignore him and call out, "Hey Gigi! Get in here, cuteness. Daddy has to implant a permanent good memory."

There's a chuckle from the bedroom, whatever they're up to is no good I can tell, and then Gigi comes running out – well, more lurching like a drunken sailor, she's still getting used to running full tilt on those new legs at two-ish (Julie knows the exact age, but she says it in months, I think it's like twenty-one-point-three-five months or something, I don't know why we can't just say "she's two") and she scoots under Pete's legs and hops up on the couch between us. I put her on my lap and peer deeply into her big blues.

"Okay, I want you to remember something."

She nods. Very serious.

I lean in so our eyes are almost touching. "For the rest of your life."

She nods again. Giggles.

"Okay, ready? Daddy loves you more than anything in the world. Will you remember that?"

"Yup." And she laughs and tries to scooch down and get back to whatever embarrassing thing they were doing to Bobo.

"No. Wait. Gigi, tell me who *you* love more than anything in the world."

She puts a finger to her forehead, thinking. Smiles. "Mommy!"

"Okay. That's fair. Acceptable answer. And who do you love *second* most?"

She bops my nose with a finger. "Daddy!"

"All right, good. Now, who do you love *third* most, Uncle Pete, or Bobo? Choose your answer wisely, young Jedi."

She looks over at Pete, who's pointing to himself emphatically, literally begging to be third-most-loved by her highness Gigi, and she gets that little mischievous grin on her face and squints at him, and whispers, "Bobo?"

Pete's face contorts into something from a cheap soap opera, like the exaggerated shock of being spurned by a true love, like "*After everything I've done for you?!*" yeah, he's really laying it on thick, and Gigi is giggling her head off, and then Pete gets fake angry, and Gigi squeals in delight and runs away, because she knows this means a race around the apartment. So they scamper through the living room to the kitchen and back, the princess hunted by the big scary monster, and then back to the kitchen, and-

Bonk!

"Oh shit."

I rush into the kitchen, and sure enough, Gigi's laying there on the floor holding her head, she must've hit it on the dishwasher again, and- "Yikes! Blood! Pete, hand me that towel!"

Gigi's crying turns into ear-piercing shrieks at the sight of her own blood, so as I sit there and huddle her close and hold a towel with pressure against her noggin and rock her back and forth, Hannah and Bobo come running out.

"Oh my God." Pete laughs. A big, deep, Pete belly laugh. He won't stop.

I look up at him. "Hey, dude, what's your problem? This could be seriou-" then I see Bobo. "Yikes. What the hell happened to you?"

I don't know why I even asked, it's obvious what happened to Bobo, what those two "angels" were up to in the bedroom: it's haircut night at *Salon de Collins*. Poor Bobo is standing there with giant patches of fur missing, randomly, all over his body.

Pete gently takes the scissors away from Hannah, and Gigi laughs, between her sobs and those eyes so heavy with little toddler tears. Bobo shuffles over to us and puts his hand to his mouth, uh-oh, he looks like he's going to do the *eat-his-own-flesh-and-regurgitate-it-on-her-to-heal-her* thing.

"Dude! Bobo, no. She's fine. God, once was enough with that. Here, look, she's fine."

I pull the towel away, and wouldn't you know: not only is there no blood leaking out from her cut…

There's no cut.

And I literally watch as the bump on her head slowly disappears.

"Huh. Hey, Pete. You seeing this?"

"Yeah. You passed on your freaky Bobo healing genes to her. I guess that's a good thing."

Hmmm. Pete's right, of course, Gigi's got half my Chip-Bobo genes. Bobo gave them to me when he molded his regurgitated flesh to my ankle stump (giving me this stupid furry foot), and I passed them down to Gigi. But… is that a good thing? What if she grows up with a furry foot? A say a silent prayer for her not to grow up with a furry foot. Please, God, in your infinite power, spare my child the curse of the furry foot. Well, it's not exactly a curse, but it's embarrassing. Please let her be embarrassed throughout her life by normal embarrassing stuff. Not an embarrassing furry foot. Thank you in advance, God.

Gigi looks up at me, smiling now, wiping the tears away with her shirt sleeves, and I wonder if she's got the telepathy thing too, not sure if that would be better or worse than a furry foot. But she just stands up, so we're eye-to-eye now, and says, "Go see Old Man."

"No, honey. We don't need to see Old Man. Your boo-boo's all gone. See?" And I lift her chubby fingers up to touch her own healed head. "Feel that? It's gone."

"No go see Old Man?"

"Nope. You don't need Old Man to kiss your boo-boo. There is no boo-boo."

"No go see Old Man?" This time she's asking it with a quaver in her voice, lips trembling, more tears welling in her eyes, goddammit, I already know where this is going.

"No, honey, no tears. Please. We can't see Old Man. He's, uh… working. He's very busy. Busy, busy, busy."

But she's not listening anymore. She's wailing like she hit her head on ten dishwashers, she wants to see Old Man and that's that. Dammit. Oh, and great, now look, Hannah's crying for Old Man too. Wonderful. And wait - *Bobo?* Bobo's big, black Bambi eyes are welling up too.

"Oh for Christ's sake, Bobo. Seriously? You don't even know what they're crying about."

Through the wailing and the pleading and the barely-controlled chaos, I spy Pete tapping on his phone. "It's no use. I surrender. I'm fetching us an Uber over to the ITA."

Yup. The ITA.

If you haven't guessed by now, about Gigi's Old Man crush? Yeah.

It's Nikola Tesla.

So I guess we're taking them all over to Room 3327 of the New Yorker Hotel for a little jump into the INTERDIMENSIONAL TRANSFER APPARATUS. Great. "Pete, you're just doing this because you couldn't bear to lose another game of Madden, aren't you?"

He responds rhetorically. "You'd rather to listen to this for three hours?"

As we bundle them up and make our way down the stairs, this odd family, the Masters of Interdimensional Travel and their two kids, and an alien disguised as a hoodie-wearing, way-too-hairy grade schooler (though not quite as hairy at the moment!), I realize *this* is the book Pete was talking about. It started at this exact moment, right now. Without reading a single email I know the FBI wants me to continue this story, the crazier the better, because it'll help perpetuate the myth that none of this is real, that Nikola Tesla couldn't possibly have invented a dimensional portal in his hotel room in New York City, and that there couldn't possibly be villains like WHO, or strange multidimensional abominations like the

Blue Juice, and most of all, it couldn't possibly be true that some doofus named Chip Collins has saved them all, that there have been moments when all of reality has depended on the actions of a man who can't even match his own socks.

We pile into the car, buckle the kids into their car seats, and Gigi looks up at me, through the little face opening in her parka, snowflakes melting on her eyelashes. "Go see Old Man."

"Yes, my little babushka. We're going to see the Old Man. And he'll kiss your boo-boo."

She smiles, and sighs, and whispers, "Tell me."

Which means tell her the whole story, the whole crazy epic tale with Tesla. She never gets tired of hearing it. And so I begin. "Once upon a time there were two regular guys, Daddy and Uncle Pete, this is way before you kids by the way, anyway I was a security guard at an old FBI building – which is not as glamorous as it sounds – and I found the lost journal of Old Man. His name is Nikola Tesla, the world's most amazing inventor ever. In his hotel room, because of course that's where you build this kind of thing, he created a special doorway to other parallel dimensions, the INTERDIMENSIONAL TRANSFER APPARATUS, and me and Uncle Pete sort of locked ourselves inside. So we needed to find Old Man to help us get home, but along the way we met Bobo, and Meg, and we had to defeat a bad guy-"

She giggles. "WHO!"

"Yes, that's right, baby. WHO. This very bad man – who unfortunately reminded me very much of Santa Claus – was trying to get rid of all the universes except one. What an evil, silly man! Anyway, during a fight with him, I got my foot chopped off, and Bobo, two of them, chewed their own hands off and helped me grow back my foot."

"Fuwwy!"

"M-hmm. Daddy's furry foot. Anyway, he gave me, and I guess you now, healing ability, oh and also telepathy. So we fought this guy WHO and his minions in the Epic Battle for the

Multiverse, and because we are not only your daddies but big, amazing heroes, we won and saved everything."

"Yay! Gigi save too!

"Not exactly, but, uh, sure. Maybe someday you'll save everything too. Why not? Anyway, after a while, Uncle Pete disappeared, and we found out it was because of some icky blue goop. The Blue Juice. It was gross."

"Ewww! Gwoss!"

"Yes, gwosser than gwoss. So me and Gina, you know her, right?"

"Aunt Gina!"

"Yup. Me and Aunt Gina had to visit ABBA the Cockroach King, and learn how to use the telepathy Bobo gave me, and save Uncle Pete. All of the Uncle Petes. Infinite Uncle Petes. Oh, and Albert Einstein, too. But before we could say we won again, Daddy had to play President of the United States, and with the help of all of his friends, make the Blue Juice go away forever. And then me and Mommy got married – again – and had you."

I look down with a sappy grin on my face, and… she's fast asleep.

My phone beeps, it's Julie sending me a photo of her and Meg and now Gina Phillips doing shots. Oh boy. "Hey dude. Look who they found." I show him the phone but it's off already, so he hits the home button and notices the date. "Hey. It's February 29th. Leap year." He slaps me on the back. "Happy birthday, Clarence Chip Collins."

Oh. I don't know if I ever told you: leap year is my birthday. I do the math in my head – dividing by four? It hurts – and proclaim, "Ah! Nine leap years since 1984. I'm nine."

"Sounds right. You act nine." He glances at Hannah, also asleep. "You know what, tomorrow we'll get an ice cream cake with crunchies for you, promise."

Hmmm. That reminds me. "Hey. Remember the first time we hit the ITA? It was on your thirtieth birthday."

• • •

And that's when I have the thought, the one I have at the start of every one of these books, a thought that makes me want to laugh, and cry, and scream, and run away while screaming at the same time. (And maybe, must maybe, shit in my pants.) Pete's staring at me with the same exact look, and I know he's thinking the same exact thing, as we're about to jump into the ITA on my birthday during a leap year, just like when we jumped into the ITA on his birthday and shit started exploding immediately. And I say the words out loud, but I know we both only half-believe them:

"Don't worry, dude. Nothing's going to go wrong this time."

2. THE OLD MAN

"No. Are you insane?"

"Come on, Fred. You did it for us before."

"I did it to appease you, to stop you from reminding me for the zillionth time that you saved the multiverse. I did it ONCE. It was not meant to set a precedent."

"And yet it has."

"No. And that's final. And you're supposed to be writing a book. Didn't you get all the emails?"

Fred, my boss's boss, is standing there, tapping his foot, red-faced, in the middle of the New Yorker Hotel's third floor Room 3327, a.k.a. the INTERDIMENSIONAL TRANSFER APPARATUS (in all caps of course), a.k.a. the bridge to the Starship Enterprise, while Gigi and Hannah and Bobo run around his legs giggling, actually they're running around all the Shrug Team's legs, the guys in the white suits who always seems to be milling around aimlessly, and as a group they sort of shrug on cue, and drift away into the corners of the room, I assume waiting for the command from Fred to, once again, get him a cup of coffee so he can allow two children and an officially-nonexistent alien to take an unauthorized trip into the most dangerous device on the planet.

I pick up *The Journal of Nikola Tesla, 1941 - .* "Oh, I'll need this to let him know we're coming."

He slaps the journal down. "You are NOT going in there! Get out of here. Now."

Pete winks at me and pats him on the shoulder. "If you say so, boss." He points down to the kids and Bobo. "We'll be back at eleven to pick up the little angels."

We grin at each other and leave the hotel room as Fred shouts after us, and the hundred or so deadbolts lock him in with our human tornadoes. I mean angels.

We stand right outside the door. "You're a genius, Pete."

"I know. Now, how long do you give him?" As he says this, the inevitable wailing begins.

"Fred? Ten bucks he doesn't last thirty seconds."

"I say he lasts more than thirty seconds but less than a minute."

Forty-five seconds later, the door swings open, and I hand Pete a ten-dollar bill, and Fred grumbles, "I can't believe I haven't been fired already, but this will certainly do it."

"I love you, Fred."

"Well I don't love you right now. Either of you. Let's get this over with."

He guides us back to the StarCloset thingy, and one of the Shrug Team guys, I swear for the first time ever, actually speaks. "Uh, Mr. Morris, sir? Isn't this when you ask us to go out and get you a cup of coffee?"

Fred's in too much of a flustered rush, ignoring him, looking down at his watch. "All right. You have five minutes. I'm not kidding. In and out. Say your hellos and your goodbyes and that's it. You hear me?"

The Shrug Team guy tugs at his shirt sleeve gently. "Uh, Mr. Morris. Sir. Shouldn't they at least have clean suits on?"

Fred realizes he's broken the unspoken Shrug Team protocol, so he shouts, "Out. You and the others. Go get me a cup of coffee!"

The guy looks at me and whispers, "that's more like it," and him and the team skedaddle (God I love that word, *skedaddle*, wait is that even an actual word?) and Fred pushes us all into the StarCloset. Then, with that familiar whoosh, the ITA door opens, and – without anyone hitting their heads maybe for the first time ever – we're inside. Fred still looks pissed as the door closes, but Gigi waves bye-bye to him, and the last thing I see is Fred's mouth curling up into a grin, and his little piggies waving back, like a favorite uncle to his favorite niece.

That's Fred. He's the man. The FBI's lucky to have him, even if he ultimately breaks every single one of their rules for me, and puts the fate of the multiverse in jeopardy just because he's a pushover.

So anyway, the ITA hallway is exactly as we left it, as it always is, grayer than the grayest gray, but strangely homey now, like that cabin up in Maine that freaked the living shit out of me the first time I stayed there, but became almost welcoming the more I went back. Like a home away from home. Almost. Don't get carried away, Chip. Remember how many times you've almost died in here, Chip.

Gigi and Hannah are clapping their hands in excitement and anticipation, so I pull out the journal and write:

> *Nikola – your number one fans are here. Waiting. You better come soon or I think their heads are going to explode.*

And before I can even start waiting for a written response, the door, the same door we just came through in 2020, whooshes open to another era, the mid-nineteen-forties, and the real-life, actual Nikola Tesla steps through. Or more accurately hobbles through, slouched over, sporting a cane. I wonder how old he is now, it's hard to keep track because time stops in here in the ITA, but proceeds normally in his dimension. Is he ninety? Ninety-one? I mean, I'm not sure it matters, he's reeeaaaallly old either way. Now, when I look close, I hate to say this – he's maybe *too* old.

But he sheds at least a dozen years when he spots Gigi and Hannah, a smile splashing across his face so wide it's reaching back to his ears, and his eyes light up like the grandpa whose granddaughters just scored their first soccer goal.

"Old Man! Old Man! Old Man!" the girls are chanting, hugging his legs and reaching up. He can't possibly pick them up, so instead he rests his cane on the floor and plops down, leaning against the wall next to me and Pete. The girls giggle and show him their imaginary forehead boo-boos, and he kisses them and makes them all go away.

While they sit down and snuggle next to him, Tesla turns to me, tousles my hair, and gives me a sly grin. "Master Chip. Good to see you. They are getting so big! Do you remember the first time I met Gigi?"

Super-Quick Sub-story: The First Time Nikola Tesla Met Gigi Collins

So the last time Fred let us do this, Gigi and Hannah were just past being babies, they couldn't quite walk yet, so maybe ten months? Again with the months. I have no idea. Anyway, Tesla's doting on them, and they're loving it, goo-gooing and baa-baaing, and having absurd little gibberish conversations with him about quantum string theory or how to make dark matter, and suddenly Gigi looks like she's having a brainstorm, and raises her finger into the air.

"Chip! I think your little one is about to speak her first word! I wonder if it will be 'superconductor'! Or 'trigonometry'! Or 'electromagnetic'!"

Gigi reaches out for his hand, totters over to his ear, and whispers, "Shit."

Without even looking, Tesla's hand shoots out at a million miles an hour and smacks me. "Chip!"

"What?!"

"What are you teaching this innocent child?"

"It wasn't me! I swear! I've been really good around her! Perfect actually! I swear!"

"Do not lie to me, young man."

"I'm not lying! Maybe she picked it up on a TV show, or Pete. Yeah, it was Pete."

Pete punches me in the shoulder. "Hey! Don't throw me under the bus! I'm not teaching your kid how to say 'shit.'"

"You say 'shit' all the time. Like every other word!"

"Bullshit!"

"See?"

Tesla slams his hand on the wall. "Silence!" And he looks around, and something's revealing itself to him, I can tell, his little Tesla coils are burning, but I can't tell what it is, until his eyes stop on Bobo.

Blink. Blink.

"YOU!"

Bobo, eyes bigger and sadder than ever, whispers, *"SHITBIT?"*

I laugh. I can't help it. Bobo taught Gigi her first word and it was "shit." I pat him on the head, yeah, kinda proud of him, I'll admit. "Dude. What does 'shitbit' even mean?"

"Enough!" Tesla's ripping pissed now. "You will strike that word from your vocabulary around these children! Do you hear me?"

The three of us, even Bobo, nod.

"Very well. Now," he takes a few deep breaths, and turns to the girls. "Who would like to hear a story?"

They're in complete awe, like he's a god – which of course, he is – perfectly silent for the first time in their lives, with rapt attention, as Tesla launches into…

Even-More-Super-Quick Sub-Sub-Story:
The Story of Arthur the Aardvark

"Woah, Nikola, hold on. Are you talking about the kids' show? There's already an Arthur the Aardvark."

"No, there is not."

"Yes there is. I read the books when I was a kid and watched the show. It's from way back in the seventie- oh. Never mind. Continue."

"Ahem. Once upon a time, there was an aardvark named Arthur. He ate ants, as all aardvarks do, of course, but he also ate… rice pudding!"

Gigi and Hannah babble in unison, "Pudda!"

"Yes! Now, the other aardvarks scowled and shunned poor Arthur. So Arthur decided to make a huge batch of rice pudding, and open a little cafe, and when he served his rice pudding, the other aardvarks exclaimed in glee, 'this is delicious!' and they lifted him on their shoulders and paraded him around the village as a hero!"

Gigi and Hannah do the clap hands thing and shimmy around, this is clearly the best story ever told, but me and Pete are like, "uh, is that it?"

"Of course that is it."

"I swear I was waiting for Arthur to invent a Resonant Tunneling Diode or a Micro Dark Matter Time Loop or some shi- I mean *stuff*. That story was something me and Pete would come up with in college, after, uh… partaking."

"What is meant by 'partaking?'"

"Uh, nothing. Okay, kiddos, say your goodbyes to the old man, we gotta get going."

"Ol-ma! Ol-ma! Ol-ma!"

"Aww, cute. I think they're calling you Old Man. And don't worry, Nikola, I won't say 'shit' in front of them ever again."

"Shit! Shit! Shit!"

"Oops."

Okay, where the hell was I, I'm like trapped three levels deep in this story. Oh yeah, so we're sitting here again with Tesla, Gigi and Hannah and Bobo surrounding him, they can sort of talk now, so they're chanting "Story time! Story time! Story time!" like they're sitting around the campfire waiting for the tribe's witch doctor to tell them how the Earth Mother created the fires in the sky, and Tesla breaks out another one of his absurd animal stories, this one's about a raccoon that can fly. Gigi and Hannah think it's even better than the aardvark rice pudding story, but even they can't resist the soothing, grandpa-like voice of Nikola Tesla, and before he can say "The End," they're fast asleep again.

Tesla smiles and whispers, "They really are angels, my friends." He gingerly pushes them aside, and rises, silently, kissing his hand and then touching their heads with the kiss. He nods at us, and we understand that this is goodbye, for tonight at least, and he takes the few steps to our home doorway and enters zero-zero-zero-zero. The little whoosh threatens to wake the kids, but Tesla opens the door ever-so-slowly, smiles and winks back at us. Then he turns and bends down a little, and shuffles back through the open door into 1947, and-

"Wait! Gigi! No!"

Gigi, suddenly awake, in a flash and a blur, runs right between his legs, giggling.

Into 1947.

Uh-oh.

Tesla turns on his heels back to us, a look of absolute terror in his eyes, the first time I've seen him so afraid, and we whisper the word to each other, the forbidden word we never thought we'd say: "Paradox!"

Pete looks between Tesla and me, puzzled. "*Paradox.* What is that, your secret word?"

"Gigi. Stop and listen. Come back out here to Daddy. Slowly. Pretty please."

She runs back out and jumps into my arms. "Come, Daddy! Come home with Old Man!"

Pete reaches out, grabs my chin, and turns my face to him. "Dude. You're white as a ghost. It's scaring me. What the hell is a paradox?"

"It's… it's… Nikola. You tell him."

Tesla takes a deep breath. "Master Pete. When Chip and I first returned home following the Epic Battle for the Multiverse, after you stayed behind to live with Meg, I explained to Chip that we needed to enter our home dimension *separately*. You see, we are both from this dimension, but I entered in 1943, and Chip entered in 2015. The INTERDIMENSIONAL TRANSFER APPARATUS **cannot resolve that temporal contradiction**. Two beings from the same home dimension, but different points on the timeline, cannot enter that home dimension simultaneously. They cannot logically exist at the same point in time. It creates a paradox." He sighs, defeated. "Gentlemen, the moment she stepped through my legs, into my timeline…"

He falters and leans against the doorway, "…**Gigi created a paradox.**"

Gigi jumps off my lap and bolts through his legs again. "Gigi make paradox!" She points out to Hannah. "Hannah make paradox?" So of course Hannah runs into Tesla's hotel room, too, I don't know, is she doubling the paradox? Oh great, now they're taking turns, running in and out between Tesla's legs. "Gigi make paradox!" "Hannah make paradox!" "Gigi make paradox!" "Hannah make paradox!"

"Stop!" The girls freeze in place. Pete stands up, pulls them out, holding them back as they try to create more paradoxes. "Nikola. Is a paradox bad?"

"Yes, Master Pete. Very bad."

"How bad is very bad?"

Tesla looks around for something simple to illustrate how bad it is, I mean it's me and Pete he's trying to explain this to, gotta keep it basic, and suddenly he wanders off into his hotel room.

"Hey! Nikola! Where are you goi- Oh."

He's back, holding a sleeve of Ritz crackers.

"Ritz crackers? Cool. That doesn't seem very bad."

He shakes his head, holds up the sleeve horizontally. "Gentlemen: imagine the first cracker in this sleeve is 1947. And the last cracker in this sleeve is 2020. Gigi just stepped onto the first cracker, 1947, even though she *belongs* on the last cracker, 2020. A paradox. It cannot exist. There is no logical mathematical solution to a paradox."

"Uh, so?"

"In order to resolve something that cannot exist, the paradox will attempt to bring Gigi back to the year she belongs, from 1947 forward to 2020. From the first cracker to the last cracker. Like this." He smashes the sleeve together, so the first cracker meets the last cracker. The whole thing splits open and all of the crackers dissolve to dust. "And what are we left with?"

"Crumbs?"

"Even less than crumbs, Chip. It is a total collapse of the timeline. Of all the timelines, throughout the multiverse. We are left with… nothing."

"Yikes. So what do we do, just stand here and wait for a few minutes to see if we turn to crumbs?'

It takes a few moments, Tesla's still in shock, trying to figure something out that can't be figured out, but then I see his brain kicking into overdrive. Oh yeah. He's thinking of something. He's always thinking of something. Always coming up with a plan. I breathe a little easier, knowing that the next word out of his mouth will probably make this whole mess go away.

"Yes."

"That's it, Nikola? 'Yes?' Yes what? Yes you have a solution?"

"Yes, we wait for a few minutes to see if the entire multiverse collapses."

"But-" And for the first time in my life, I can't speak, I don't have a wise-ass retort, or a blubbering tear-filled rant, I mean, what can I say? What's left to say? I look down at my beautiful kid, and Pete's beautiful kid, these innocent little angels me and my idiot friend have put into harm's way, the ultimate harm's way, and then a thought even more terrifying than that pops into my head, and I manage to croak to Pete…

"Dude, if the multiverse collapses, Julie and Meg are gonna be soooo pissed."

3. I AM THE WORST FATHER IN THE HISTORY OF THE MULTIVERSE.

From: Chip Collins
To: Julie Taylor
Date: February 29, 2020 8:19pm
Subject: I am the worst father in the history of the multiverse.

Hey Julie,

Okay, so the good news first:
The multiverse didn't collapse. Well, not yet.

The bad news?
I have pigeon shit on my head.

No, really, it gets much, much worse babe, the bad news is truly
awful, but I figured I'd start off easy, with a little pigeon shit joke,
to kind of build up to the slow reveal of what's really going on.
Not that the pigeon thing was a joke like made-up-ha-ha, it really
did happen, the stupid bird pooped directly on my head while it
was sailing through the blue skies of New York City, dropping its
dung-missile with absolutely uncanny aim. I just thought that
might help delicately introduce the true nature of how fucked we

are, how you may never see any of us again, how our dimension might not even exist anymore, at least the 2020 version of it, and how the whole fabric of the multiverse is starting to unravel and we have no fucking clue how to stop it.

Oh, whoops, I kind of just told you the whole awful thing anyway, didn't I?

All right then. Yes. I am writing to you to apologize, once again, for being me, and this time it's worse – no, it's the worst – because our progeny is with me, our little bumpkin-head Gigi, and my idiocy has reached new and unparalleled heights (or is it depths?), and I admit that through two whole novel-length books, I have not really learned anything. I mean, I've learned about love, a whole lot about that, more than could fill a thousand books, but nothing practical, like how not to be a bonehead, or prevent easily-preventable things like multiverse-destroying paradoxes from happening.

I'm sorry.

I can't take any of it back, but maybe by hearing the whole story you'll find it in your heart to forgive me. (Yes, that was rhetorical. Even if you still exist, you will never forgive me. And rightly so.) Anyway, here's what happened:

1. Gigi walks into dimension #234,698,594,394,683, a.k.a, home, but between Tesla's legs, into the year 1947. This creates a paradox. We don't know what a paradox looks like – just the metaphor of a sleeve of Ritz crackers smashing together – or how fast it is, or really anything about it yet. I was sincerely hoping all we had to do was apologize politely to the paradox, and it would forgive us with a hearty, "off you go, no worries mates," but I tried that, and nothing happened.

2. We wait for a few minutes to see if the multiverse collapses. It doesn't. So far okay. Maybe this paradox thing isn't so bad after all.

3. Tesla closes the door, and asks me to try it. I open it, expecting 2020 of course, but no. 1947. Fuck. (I don't actually say "fuck," come on, give me some credit, Gigi's with us.) Pete's like, "maybe you're doing it wrong," so I'm like "you try it, Mister Do-Right," so he does, and same thing. 1947. Ugh. So I'm like, "See?" and he's like, "Don't get all smarmy with me, dude. Your kid broke the multiverse, not mine."

"Oh. Really. That's how it's going to be. *My* kid broke it."

"She did."

I go to shove him, but stop. "Actually, you're right." I turn to Gigi. "Bad Gigi. You broke the multiverse."

She just looks up at me, doe-eyed. "Muttiver?"

"Whatever. You're just a kid. You can't even control your own bowels yet. Although come to think of it, neither can I. Okay, next."

4. So we try it every which way, we even have Bobo do it, and every time… 1947. Bobo's like, "STUCKFUCK," and we all practically shove our fists into his mouth to keep Gigi and Hannah from hearing it and adding it to their rapidly-growing vocabulary of swearwords.

5. I give up. The paradox has us stuck here in 1947.

So.

1947 it is.

"Okay, Nikola, which chair do I sit in while I wait five more minutes for you to figure this out?" I plop myself down in the one by the big desk, the cozy-looking high-backed leather arm chair, which I immediately regret, because this one appears to my nose to be Tesla's farting chair.

"Chip. I would not get too comfortable. I would plan, in fact, to be here for quite some time. Until we establish the scope of the paradox, its rate of speed, and devise a possible solution."

"Don't have to ask me to get out of that chair twice." I bound up, letting poor Gigi and Hannah climb onto it instead. They don't seem to smell the old man's past three decades of digested meals, or don't mind it at least. Good for them. "So, Nikola, if we're here for the duration, we're going to have to fit in with the locals. Any words I need to know other than *keen*, and *berries*, and *jake*, and *bee's knees*?"

"*BEEZ NEEZ.*"

"Crap. Hey Bobo, look over there!" I throw a paperclip across the room and Bobo is distracted just long enough to forget he was about to repeat *BEEZ-NEEZ* a million times until we all strangled him. (It's a little trick I picked up over the past couple of years. Pretty proud of that one, actually.) I get an approving nod from Pete.

Tesla wags his finger. "No, Chip. You don't need to learn any mid-twentieth century vernacular…"

"Cool."

"…because we won't be leaving this room."

"Woah. *Not* cool. What the hell- HECK, I mean, what the heck?"

Pete points out the window. "Yeah. We're gonna need some fresh air. Soon. No offense."

"I suppose I have never had a reason to tell you this, gentlemen, why we cannot leave this room, but now I must: Master Chip, do we come from the same dimension?"

"Ooh, a quiz! My final answer is 'Yes.' How may points do I get?"

He ignores me and turns to Pete. "And Master Pete, does each dimension have its own, single timeline?"

Pete's still staring outside. Shrugs. "Why are you asking *me?*"

"It does. And while on the same timeline, Chip, if I were to affect a future event from here in 1945, say by convincing your mother to move away from New York before she met your father-"

"Hey! Why would you do that? That's just mean! Why wouldn't you tell *Pete's* mother to do that?"

Pete whirls around. "Hey!"

"Men! It was just an example. I would never do such a thing. But if I did, what would happen?"

It begins to dawn on me, the terrible problem presented by different people on different parts of the same timeline using the ITA. I had honestly never thought about it. "If you convinced my mom to move away, and she didn't meet my dad… I wouldn't be here, would I?"

Tesla raises a finger. "Exactly."

"So Nikola, what are you telling me?"

He looks sheepishly around the room, then back to me. And for the first time, I really look around at all the little details, the empty Ritz cracker boxes, the clothes piled to the ceiling, the stacks of newspapers, and I smell the unmistakable smell of an old man who takes care of himself, alone, in this room, and never leaves. "You've avoided creating ripples in the future timeline of our dimension by never leaving this room, Nikola? You don't go outside? Ever?"

He shakes his head.

"How do you eat? Do your laundry? Drop your friends off at the pool?"

"My… friends at the pool?"

I point to my butt. "You know…"

"Ah. Another colorful slang term from your era. My toilet works, Master Chip. As for food and outside utilities, I have found nearby dimensions using the ITA to fill those needs, dimensions where my presence does not pose a future threat. In fact, I have made quite a name for myself in several, amassing enough wealth to pay off the rent on this room in a lump sum for the next thirty years. The New Yorker Hotel was thrilled with the cash infusion, and it gave them reason to ignore the remaining inquiries from the FBI. They haven't asked a question since. Chip, listen: since my return, I understood that dimension #234,698,594,394,683 had gone on without me, believing me dead. Your own records indicate as such. So I have lived here, occasionally sneaking out at night to feed my pigeons, instructing the hotel employees to never interact with me, or disturb this room, even for cleaning."

"I can see that." I turn to look around some more but then turn back. "Hey, wait. *'Pose a future threat?'* You mean, you've been holed up in this room, alone, for two years now, just to protect *us?*"

He smiles and puts his hand on my shoulder. "It has been my honor. Look, just look at your beautiful children."

"No, that's bullshit." I look over at Gigi and Hannah. "Sorry girls." Back to Tesla. "But it is. We've been keeping you a *prisoner* here, all alone-"

"I have my pigeons. And like I said, I spend as much time as I like in my neighboring dimensions. Do not feel sorry for me."

"I don't feel sorry for you. You should've told me-"

A rumble shakes the room.

Tesla scratches his chin. "Hmmm."

"God, Nikola, can I just tell you I really don't like it when you say "hmmm" anymore? It's become this cue that something really, really bad is going to happen. Like every single time lately. I won't even say it anymore, it gives me the heebie-jeebies. Now what the hell was that?"

"HEEB-JEEB."

"Shut up, Bobo. Nikola – what was that?"

Tesla cautiously steps towards the ITA doorway. Leans down. Then kneels at the side of the doorway and squints. "Hmmm."

"Nikola!"

"I apologize. Here, at the corner of the INTERDIMENSIONAL TRANSFER APPARATUS doorway. The wallpaper is peeling back."

"Uh. So? This place isn't exactly in mint condition. No offense."

"None taken. But Master Chip, please… take a look for yourself."

Julie, it's one of those moments from the movies. Everyone stops what they're doing, Bobo stops picking lint off his fur, Gigi and Hannah stop playing *who-can-be-more-annoying* (a game I taught them, btw, I'm the master of course, but you knew that already), Pete just slowly turns to watch me as I plod the death-march to witness something terrible, from a nightmare, something I do NOT want to see, but I *have* to see. I lean down, eyes shut now, man is there a way this can be something quick and painless, something that'll answer our big question, which is "how the fuck do we get home?"

I slowly open my eyes, and…

"Yup. Peeling wallpaper. No biggie. Hey Pete, pass me some tape."

Tesla doesn't even say a word. He just pushes my head down a little, so I can see from his angle.

Oh no.
Oh my God no.

Have you ever wondered what a paradox looks like?
Stop wondering. And put on your adult diapers.

4. FIVE THINGS A PARADOX LOOKS LIKE

From: Chip Collins
To: Julie Taylor
Date: February 29, 2020 8:19pm
Subject: Five things a paradox looks like.

Hey Julie,

"It's like… It's like…"

It's no use. This paradox thing looks like… everything… and nothing. There aren't words. But while Tesla runs out to check our neighboring dimensions, you know me, I'm Mister Word Guy, so I'll give it a shot anyway:

Five Things a Paradox Looks Like:

1. Okay the obvious first: it's orange. There's an orange glow coming from behind the peeling wallpaper. Not exactly what you'd expect, you'd expect it to be plaster and lathe, or some old,

criminally sub-standard electrical wiring from the turn of the century, but so far not too weird, just an orange glow. Then I peek a little deeper inside and the weird starts.

2. A mirror. That's the first thing I think when I really look inside the little inch-wide abyss. Like I'm looking at myself. But not just myself *now*. Myself yesterday. And the day before that. Stretching out way back to when I was a baby (I was a pretty damn cute baby, actually, that part isn't so traumatic), and way forward to me being an old man and then a skeleton in the dirt (that part is the traumatic part).

3. That scene from *2001: A Space Odyssey* where Dave goes all trippy and enters the psychedelic world of the black monolith thing. Like I finally understand that scene for the first time. You know what? I'm adding a star. I always gave that movie three stars because it was just too fucking confusing, but now I'm giving it four. I know I shouldn't be worried about star ratings at the moment, but thought you'd want to know. Like if you were on the fence about renting it, I'd say at this point go for it. Or just look into the paradox like me and you'll get the whole thing at once and save yourself the five bucks.

4. Sesame chicken. Listen, I know that doesn't make sense. But it just does. It looks like sesame chicken. If I wasn't so freaked out I might even say it looks kind of delicious. Like sesame chicken can be *meh* or mind-blowing, and this would definitely be leaning toward mind-blowing.

5. *Chaos.* Okay, yeah, now I think I'm getting the hang of this. Yup. Chaos. Like everything that's supposed to be in order is falling apart, across all dimensions, shooting out all over the place. I vaguely remember Tesla telling me about something called *entropy* one time, about how higher orders of complexity naturally diffuse out into lower orders of complexity based on probability

(wow, look at me, remembering technical shit!). Anyway, this looks like it's speeding up entropy. Which I guess would mean speeding up time, on its way to ultimate chaos. Wonderful. And I'm watching it happen. Zero stars for this shit. I hate this movie. I want my money back. What? I didn't pay to get in? Well fuck you, I want something for my trouble here. I don't know. Free popcorn. Hand it over, imaginary movie theater flunky guy.

Tesla reenters the room, kneels down next to me, and whispers, "It is everywhere. All dimensions. All stuck back in time. As I had feared. Did you see what I saw?"

I stop my internal argument with imaginary movie theater flunky guy and whisper back, "Entropy?"

He smiles, I guess even in this moment of absolute terror, he's delighted that his ever-dense protege Chip has actually had an insight, actually remembered some morsel of something intelligent his mentor tried to cram into his neanderthal brain. "Exactly, Chip. I saw the same. The paradox is beginning to accelerate entropy to infinite speed. This acceleration will compress time, so that my 1947 and your 2020 meet – collapsing the timeline entirely. To our perception, it will appear that time will move faster and faster, and we will age rapidly, until we reach 2020…"

"…the hard way. Like the Ritz crackers."

"Exactly again." He measures the tear in the wallpaper with a ruler. Waits a minute. Measures it again. "The rate of paradox expansion is accelerating, as predicted. We won't have much time – pardon the pun – to fix this, Master Chip. Now, were there any other clues revealed? Did you see anything else when peering into the paradox?"

"Yeah. Sesame chicken. Kind of."

Pete snorts.

"Hey dude. I'm trying to describe the indescribable. You want to see for yourself? You think you can give it a better description?"

He finally looks back from the window. Annoyed. "Nah, Your psychedelic mind-blowing whatever blah, blah, blah sesame chicken is fine. Listen, we've got another problem."

"Oh, for crying out loud. What now?"

"Look." He points outside.

Great. You know, I should know better, the minute you think you've seen the worst, most horrific thing ever, something else even more diarrhea-inducing piles on, just to smush your face in it. Goddammit. So I get up and do another death march over to Pete, and Gigi and Hannah slide off the farting chair and want us to pick them up to see, so there we all are, the four of us, and Bobo, peeking out the third-floor hotel room window down onto 34th Street in midtown Manhattan, 1947.

"So what am I looking for?"

Gigi giggles and points. "Old Man!"

And yeah, there's an old man with a cane, taking forever to cross Eighth Avenue, cars are honking at him, cabbies are yelling their old-timey slang at him, like "watcha think ya doin' there palsy-walsy?", I almost want to laugh, what's the big deal – until he turns his head and looks straight up at us. Right into my eyes. I gasp.

Tesla joins us at the window, and Pete answers his question before it even passes his trembling lips. "Yes, Nikola. It's you."

5. TESLA'S GHOST

From: Chip Collins
To: Julie Taylor
Date: February 29, 2020 8:19pm
Subject: Tesla's Ghost

Hey Julie,

"Temporal entropic anomaly."

"Tesla's Ghost."

"Temporal entropic anomaly."

"Tesla's Ghost. It sounds better."

Pete steps between me and Tesla. "Shut up. Both of you. Nikola, whatever it is, what does it mean?"

Tesla takes a deep breath, then thinks twice about giving our little group of toddlers (including two actual toddlers) a full explanation, and settles on this: "As I said, the paradox is accelerating the normal rate of entropy, speeding up time and collapsing the timeline, in order to resolve the temporal contradiction. It is clearly now beginning to create temporal anomalies like this."

"And in English?"

"Random events or people. Appearing outside of the ordered timeline. Like apparitions."

"See? *Tesla's Ghost.* I told you!"

Tesla ignores me, taps his chin. "It may not be random. There may be a reason this anomaly is happening at this moment in the timeline. I cannot be certain."

Pete takes the reins. "Well, there's only one way to find out." And he stuffs a kid under each arm and heads for the door.

So we cram into the elevator, Tesla's hyperventilating, he hasn't seen the outside of his hotel room for years, well, this hotel room anyway, and when we finally spill out into the lobby and make our way past the concierge desk, a woman calls out to us.

"Gentlemen! And children! May I help you? I'm the new concierge, here at your service!"

God, could she sound any more chipper? Wait. I forgot: we're in 1947. We're back in *post-World-War-Two-chipper-level-eleven* times. But we're in a rush, can't make any chipper small talk, got Tesla's Ghost to chase down. So we pretend not to notice her and skulk by, like the worst-trained bunch of spies in the world.

And that's when Pete makes the mistake.

He turns his head ever-so-slightly, to take a look at who's being so chipper. A girl, early twenties maybe, with tortoise-shell retro glasses and a jangly charm bracelet, waves at us enthusiastically.

"Aunt Barb?"

I whisper "Oh fuck" as the girl drops her pen and cocks her head and smiles that 1947 *I'm-confused-and-kinda-pissed-but-I-can't-be-rude-so-you-better-tell-me-what-the-fuck-is-going-on* smile. "Have we met, sir?"

At this point I'm whisper-shouting, "Keep walking, Pete. Keep walking. Dude. No ripples, dude. We have a timeline to keep, if you get my meaning."

But Pete's mesmerized, like he's looking back into his own past. He stops and approaches her. "Great Aunt Barb?"

She's blushing now. "My name is Barb, yes. But I assure you I'm no one's great aunt! I'm not even twenty yet!"

We're tugging Pete away, all of us, but he just keeps going. "Do you have a sister Shirley?"

Now she's looking around nervously, like The Amazing Pete-dini has peered into her brain a little too closely, it's getting weird, she's trying to attract someone over to bail her out. "Y- y- yes. And who might you be, sir?"

"Pete. Your grand-" And Tesla lunges over and slaps his hand over Pete's mouth, and I turn him a hundred and eighty degrees toward the door. "We're sorry, miss Barb person. Our friend Pete here is, uh, mentally, uh, what's the current word? *Touched.* Yes, touched. He has episodes like this. Don't be alarmed. We are, in fact, taking him for electroshock therapy at this very moment."

"Oh dear. Then let me call you all a cab." She picks up her desk phone.

"*NO!*"

"No?"

"We're, ah, if he doesn't walk there, it gets worse. He'll start claiming something crazy, like the Brooklyn Dodgers are moving to Los Angeles."

She laughs, a little shaky. "Well, *that* is craz- I mean, not sane-, um, well, I mean that just couldn't happen, obviously. All right then, gentlemen and little ladies, and, um, other little hairy boy, please, take care of your friend Pete, and you all have a wonderful day."

Whew.

So we rush out the revolving doors, into the crisp New York

City fall air. (Oh, forgot to tell you. We're in a completely different season than the one we left an hour ago. It's like early October or something. Shit's crazy. Don't ask.)

Pete's shaking his head. "Guys. Sorry. That was just… Jeez. I mean, it's her. My grandfather's sister. I knew she worked in hotels, but I never thought. She died when I was in junior high. It was rough, because she was like my one cool relative, the one who'd come over and drink perfect Manhattans and tell racy jokes to us kids, and she always had five bucks up her sleeve, and she'd slip it out from that big charm bracelet and say 'now don't spend it all on pretty girls' and pull my earlobe…"

Oh man. It looks like Pete's going to cry. Wow. He really loved Great Aunt Barb. "Hey, dude. Sorry." I go to give him a hug, and he stiff-arms me, and we get regular Pete back. "Not now, dude. I'll let you know when it's hug time. Sorry to get us off track there. Where to, Nikola?"

I take my first good look around. "Huh. Why did I expect everything to be in black and white?"

"Because you're an idiot."

And almost instantly, I feel something wet seeping into my scalp, and reach up and touch it. "Oh, come on. The FIRST thing that happens as I step out onto the streets of 1940s New York is a pigeon shits on my head."

Pete laughs. "Hey, that should make you feel comfortable. Like 'Welcome home, Chip. Don't worry, some things never change.'"

"Good point." I rub some of it off on his arm as he tries to back away. "No wonder everyone's wearing hats."

"Everyone's wearing hats because it's 1947. Come on, dude. Wake up."

Anyway, one of the pigeons lands on Tesla's arm, and he gently hands it a crumb of bread (I guess he keeps a stash in his pocket at all times for just such occasions) and strokes its wings. "Well, hello Penelope."

"Penelope Pigeon. Cute. Hey, how do you know that one's Penelope?"

"They are all Penelope."

"Oh."

Before we can speed off in the direction of Tesla's Ghost, Gigi tugs my pants leg. I crouch down. "What's up, kiddo? You missing mommy?"

"Nuts!"

Oh well. Sorry, Julie. I sincerely was checking to make sure Gigi was all there, like any normal kid, I figured she'd be starting to wonder what the fuck was going on, and where her mommy was, but there's a nut vendor right next to us on the corner, roasting the best-smelling candied cashews that have ever been smelled, and for the moment I guess nuts trumps Mommy, and I'm thinking we're all kind of hungry, because I hear the collective groan from our stomachs, and I swear to God I can sense the saliva gathering in all our mouths (except Bobo, of course. Julie, I don't even know why Bobo has a mouth. It certainly isn't to eat, I've never seen him eat anything, ever (except his own hands). And all he says are bullshit rhymes, so he doesn't really need it to talk. Anyway, another multiverse mystery for you to ponder while you wait for us to rescue 2020).

"Hey, nut guy. We'll take a big bag of the cashews." I turn to Pete. "Dude, you got any shillings?"

"We're in 1947 New York, not Medieval Europe."

"Right. How much for the nuts?"

The guy hands over a bag that would feed us for a month, and he's like, "That'll be ten cents, folks."

"What?"

"Ten cents. Okay, I'll throw in a coupla stick candies for the girls."

Wow. I don't think I've paid a dime for anything, ever. Like even a piece of Bazooka at the bodega is a quarter. So I hand the nut guy a buck and say, "keep the change," and he looks at me like I just paid his mortgage, and I give Gigi and Hannah a warm cashew each, and pop one in my mouth, and-

"Oh. My. God."

Tesla reaches out and turns my face toward him. Peers into my eyes. "Are you all right, Chip? Allergic reaction?"

"No." I hug the bag of nuts to my chest, feeling its warmth, smelling its mixture of sweet, salty, earthy goodness. "Can we live here, Nikola?" I look longingly around me, at the simplicity (and the inexpensiveness) and the sense of people being polite, and cars waiting for people to cross the street instead of trying to mow them down. I'm kidding, of course Julie, I wouldn't want to live here without you, but man, I wish you could see this. It's wild. I look at the Empire State Building, down 34th Street over on Fifth Avenue, sitting there all alone in the skyline, the only other building peeking up into the sky is the Chrysler Building. "Hey, Pete. Look at those two lonely buildings. Weird."

Pete grabs a cashew. "This is just getting weird for you now?"

So we head over to Bryant Park over on Sixth and 40th, Tesla's regular haunt for feeding his pigeons (Get it? Haunt? Tesla's Ghost?), that's his best guess at where to find his doppleganger, and yup, there he is, on Tesla's regular bench, throwing bread crusts on the ground, surrounded by like a jillion birds. Same Tesla, just older. Wait, is that even possible? Anyway he sees us, and motions us over.

I approach him (watch out for more pigeon shit, Chip!), and touch his arm. Solid. "Wait. You're not a ghost."

Even Older Tesla pokes me back with his cane. "Who said I was a ghost?"

Gigi and Hannah amble over, like two Teslas is the most normal thing in the world, and climb on to the bench on either side of him. "Hi Old Man."

He pats their heads, smiling weakly, then turns to Tesla, grave. "You were right. This is not random. I came to tell you."

Tesla nods. "That we don't have much time."

"You state the obvious, Nikola. Master Chip must be rubbing off on you."

"Hey!"

Tesla shushes me and turns back to Even Older Tesla. "I apologize. Go on."

"I came to tell you not to overlook the key to our problem. It is right under your nose."

I try to look under my nose, which is impossible really, because your nose gets in the way. That's like basic physics. Or biology. Whatever. "Right under our nose? What, are we supposed to grow mustaches or something?"

Even Older Tesla laughs a tired ancient man laugh, wheezing, like he's pretty much done listening to decades of stupid Chip jokes. "No, Master Chip. The key is…" and he trails off and closes his eyes.

I nudge his shoulder. "Did he just die?"

Pete leans in and takes a whiff or something. "Nah. Sleeping."

"So what, we stand here until he wakes up?"

Original Tesla just shrugs, which I take as a yes, and I gird myself to wait this nap out. Hopefully it's a cat nap, I'm not standing around here for forty five minutes listening to some old guy's wheezy snoring and asking Original Tesla what time it is every five seconds.

Suddenly I hear gravel crunching underfoot on the path right behind us.

We all whip around to face the intruder: it's Barb the concierge with the jangly charm bracelet, presumably on her break, looking down, walking, face buried in a cheap romance novel, trying to light a cigarette. She practically smashes into Pete and stops short, looking up, dropping her Pall Mall, all flustered. "Well. Isn't that strange. Here I was, lost in thought, thinking about poor Pete, and now here he is. Right under my nose!"

The three of us gape at each other and understand immediately, we don't even have to look back to see if Tesla's

Ghost is gone, yes he's done his job and has disappeared, and whether it makes any sense or not, which it doesn't, we know with a hundred percent certainty:

Great Aunt Barb is the key.

6. I THOUGHT YOU ALL WERE HEADING OFF TO ELECTROSHOCK THERAPY...

From: Chip Collins
To: Julie Taylor
Date: February 29, 2020 8:19pm
Subject: I thought you all were heading off to electroshock therapy…

"I- I- thought you all were heading off to electroshock therapy…" Aunt Barb is eyeing us over more skeptically now, our strange bunch.

"Uh, yeah. We're still making our way there, it's across the park over on Lex. The girls and Bobo wanted to feed the birds on the way."

"Bobo?"

"Bobbie! I meant Bobbie!" But it's too late, Bobo has taken the mention of his name as a cue and trots over and starts humping her leg while I try to pry him off. "Bad Bobbie!"

Aunt Barb is absolutely gobsmacked (god I love that word), but trying to keep her demure face on. "Ahem, isn't this a little, ah, inappropriate for a young man like yo-" and as she's saying it she tugs on his hoodie a little, and it slides off, and I try to throw it back over his head, but it's too late, she gets a good look at our "young man," the fur (fully grown back, btw), and the huge eyeballs, and the weird three-fingered hands, and yup, you guessed it: she faints.

Gigi giggles. "Barb go boom."

So we sneak Aunt Barb up to the hotel, still passed out, and while she does her *wake-up-see-Bobo-pass-out-again* routine three or four times on the fainting couch (it's right next to the farting chair), me and Pete and Tesla discuss our little revelation. (Or more accurately, Tesla starts thinking and talking and we just nod like we know what he's talking about.)

"Perhaps Aunt Barb has some form of latent power, like Gina Phillips with her telepathy…" We look over and Gigi and Hannah are poking the poor girl's face, trying to wake her up. Drool is making its way down her cheek. "Or perhaps not."

We finally get her up and semi-alert.

Pete's at her side. "Aunt Barb. We need to talk."

She thrusts the back of her hand to her forehead and wilts. "Oh dear! This is like one of those mystery capers I've read, where strange men have drugged me and taken me to their lair in the countryside, to demand a ransom… or worse!"

"Not exactly. It's not sinister at all, but definitely weirder."

"Then… you're a band of marauders, from some far-off, exotic land, waiting here for a wealthy sheik to visit this hotel, and you'll force me to seduce him or you'll kill me… and my entire family!"

"Again, not exactly."

"No! I won't tell you anything, you hear? You won't get it out of me! I'll die before I tell you that the combination to the hotel's safe is nine-sixteen-twelve– *oh dear!*"

As I mentally jot down *nine-sixteen-twelve* (Oh come on, Julie, wouldn't you be at least the teeniest bit curious what they keep in a hotel safe in 1947? Okay, okay, I mentally tore it up, jeez), anyway, this is getting nowhere, and she's threatening to pass out again, so I place her hand in mine. Then I open a little silver thread, from my mind to hers, my mind to hers, and gently, ever-so-gently, ask if I can tell her the story using telepathy. Surprisingly, and maybe because this is secretly some of the excitement and adventure she's been longing for her whole life, her eyes go from fear to surrender, to a little hint of a smile, and she nods.

And I tell her the whole absurd thing with my mind, leaving nothing out, not even the pigeon shit part (which she laughs at), and I don't hold back on the terror part, the part where none of this might exist in a little while if we don't figure out how she fits in, and not only does she stay with me, she's sort of getting into it, like she's Nancy Drew in her own dime-store novel – *The Entropy Riddle: An Aunt Barb Mystery.*

She gets to her feet, a little wobbly from all the new information. Pete takes her hands, and they smile at each other, a little more knowing between them now. Pete digs into his pocket and pulls out his keys. Hanging off the key ring is a heart, I never noticed it, an ancient-looking gold heart charm with a *T* engraved in the face. He holds it up to her charm bracelet, matching it perfectly with the heart there, a little newer-looking, but it's the same one, right down to the *T*. "You gave me this, Aunt Barb, told me to keep it safe."

"Did I ever tell you about this charm?"

Pete nods and laughs. "A million times. You said you bought it off a jeweler who said it was made a long, long time ago…"

She completes the sentence. "In some far away, exotic place. I never told you the ending, though. Mister Goldman only charged me two bucks for it, so I think he made the whole thing up." She laughs. "It's junk." She jangles it around her wrist. "But I love it. And I'm glad you saved it." And she reaches up and gives him a peck on the cheek.

And now, more chipper than ever, she shouts, "Well, fellas, where do we start?" Reaching into her gargantuan purse, she pulls out a Pall Mall and lights up. Gigi and Hannah look at her like she's an alien, and I realize I don't know if they've ever seen a cigarette. I mean, we're from 2020, right? And we don't exactly hang out in places where people smoke. Barb's a little confused. "Um, you know what they say, 'From breakfast to bedtime, Pall Malls are the smoking treat that treats you right!'"

"They really say that?"

Pete punches my arm. "1947, dude. How many times do I have to say it?" Turns to Barb. "Listen, if it's okay with you…" and she takes the hint and puts it out, and as the last little wisp of smoke dissipates, Bobo trots over and sniffs it, and pops it in his mouth. Holy shit. Wasn't I JUST saying how I've never seen Bobo eat anything? And now I finally do, and it's a cigarette butt? I'd say that doesn't make any sense, but, you know. Bobo.

Anyway, Tesla gently guides Aunt Barb to the ITA door. "Now, miss Barb, if we could, I would like you to peer into the opening down there."

"Where the wallpaper's peeling back? You know a little tape'd fix that right up. Or chewing gum. I've got a pack right here in my purse. I read that once in a book you know, Agent Drake used Wrigley's to stop the bleeding from a bullet in his arm."

"Perhaps we can try that later. But now…"

So they kneel down in front of the little tear – wait, is it my imagination, or has that tear gotten a little longer and orangier since we left? – and Aunt Barb peeks in.

"Miss Barb, can you tell me what you see?"

"Well, it's going to sound downright crazy. Oh, where are my manners? I didn't mean to say the word crazy. I'm sorry, Pete."

"Pete is not insane. We were pretending he was insane earlier to deceive you."

"Oh. Right."

"Now, what do you see?"

"It's… It's…"

"Yes? What do you see?"

"Sesame chicken?"

Pete snorts again.

She ignores him, and reaches out to touch the tear. Hesitates, her finger maybe an inch away.

"Miss Barb, I don't know if we should be touching that until I've completed my analysi-"

But Tesla cuts himself short as a little arc of energy travels from Barb's fingertip to the tear, turning it from orange to a little orange-greenish.

She chuckles. "Huh. Strange. It tingles. I feel like Flash Gordon."

Tesla gently pulls her hand back. "Interesting. May I try?" And he does the same thing, and… nothing.

I give her the slow clap. "Okay, so Aunt Barb has some kind of superpower. Awesome. Do your thing, Barb. Bring us home."

But Tesla blocks her hand. "Wait. There I something I want to try. I am formulating a theory. Pete, will you leave the room, please?"

"Cool. Chip, you watch the little demons, I'll be down at that bar across the street kicking back twenty-five-cent beers."

"No, Master Pete. Stand just outside the door. Until I call you."

"Whatever." And he skulks out of the room, forever-unsipped, insanely-cheap beers calling to him.

"Now, Miss Barb. Try that again."

She reaches out, smiling, expecting that cool little Flash Gordon energy arc, but her finger just hangs there, like a regular person finger, with no superpower at all. No tingles. Bummer.

"Well, that certainly isn't the bee's knees."

"*BEEZNEEZ.*"

I pick up and throw a paper clip across the room and Bobo blinks like he forgot he was going to say *bee's knees* a thousand times. Thank God. "Uh, hey Barb. Forgot to mention, don't talk in rhymes. Like, at all. Ever."

"Excuse me?"

"Trust me. Just trust me. Shit's crazy. Don't ask."

Gigi and Hannah look over, hearing their forbidden word, and grin and say together, "Shit."

"No. Girls, no. Sorry. Please don't say that. Bad word."

"Shit."

"No. Really. Daddy will get very angry."

They both giggle at this, man they've got me completely figured out at two years old, like I might as well permanently wear a shirt that says "Captain Pushover" on it, or maybe a tattoo on my forehead, and I can't help it, I smile back at them, those little mush faces, and suddenly a wave of something comes over me, and I'm back in the delivery room, two years ago…

"This is so beautiful, Chip, isn't it?"

"Yeah, Julie. Beautiful." But my voice is muffled, my hand is over my mouth, because this is the most disgusting thing I have ever seen, and I've seen a ton of gross shit. And once again, I have a new answer to that joke:

What's grosser than gross?
A human head trying to emerge from another human, like an
alien chestburster, with all kinds of fluids spraying everywhere,
and screaming and crying and stainless steel objects covered in
blood.

So I'm holding back my own bodily fluids, swallowing hard, damn that breakfast burrito is trying like hell to make a reappearance, and I'm sincerely wondering what people find so beautiful about this scene from a slasher horror movie, complete with the mad scientist doctor yelling something at me while my head spins and I almost hurl.

"Mister Collins!"

Oh wait, he's yelling my name. I shake myself to attention.

"Uh, sorry. What? I was just enjoying the.. (gag sounds)… beautiful… (gag sounds)..."

"It's a girl."

And he offers me this little blanket bundle with a face, and the nausea disappears, and for a moment I have the strange feeling they're giving me something that's not mine, I mean I didn't come in here with this, I don't have a receipt or anything, and you're going to let me just hold this and take it with us? Forever?

And then her eyes open.

I have never seen such big eyes.

Looking straight into my soul, those big blues.

She yawns, God she must be exhausted from her nine-month journey, and the little sound she makes is like an angel whispering my name, and we stare at each other for a moment, an eternity in that moment, and I finally understand. The word I'd been failing to grasp. I finally understand what it looks like to bring life into the world, the struggle of life to keep on trucking, to move from one generation to the next, to never give up. The word that I just couldn't get the whole morning comes barreling into me now with its full meaning, and wrapping me up like this little baby. As I step over to you, Julie, and rest wee little Gigi in your arms, I say the word like I've never meant any word before:

"Beautiful."

"Be happy Daddy."

Wait, where the hell am I? Oh, it's Gigi, patting me on the knee. Tears are streaming down my cheek.

"No, no honey. Daddy's not sad. Daddy just remembered the day you were born. They're happy tears." But as the words come out of my mouth I realize they're only half-true, that there is an incredible amount of sadness in these tears too, as I look at Gigi and Hannah and really feel for the first time a fear for their future. Fear that they'll never even get a chance to remember anything.

She hugs me. "Daddy happy now. Gigi fix."

God, Is there anything more Chip-like than blubbering and being comforted by my own two-year-old?

"Thanks, Gigi. You rock. Yeah, Daddy's A-okay now. Back to work." I give her the thumbs up, and wipe the wetness from my cheeks, and watch Tesla walk to the door and call out to the hall, "Master Pete, you may come back."

Pete strolls in, with a pint of beer in his hand.

"Dude!"

"What? Did you really expect me not to? It's a *quarter*, dude."

"So you couldn't afford two?"

He reveals his other hand from behind his back, holding a second beer. "Happy birthday, dude. It's not an ice cream cake with crunchies, but it was only a quarter." He hands them both to me. "Okay, Nikola, I'm all yours."

Tesla guides him to where he was standing before, and Aunt Barb puts her finger near the tear, and the energy arc thing happens again. "Oooh!"

Okay. So it's only Barb, and it's only when Pete's with her. Weird.

Tesla pulls Pete down to where Aunt Barb is sitting on the floor. "Yes. Just what I thought. Now Pete, put your hand on Miss Barb's."

He rests his fingers on hers, and immediately the arc flares, and the tear turns bright green. Tesla jumps up (or his version of jumping, he's ninety-one for Pete's sake) and shouts, "Chip! Now bring me the tape!"

"Wait. We're really going to fix the multiverse with scotch tape?"

"*Chip!*"

So I rush over with the tape and he pulls off a length, pressing down the peeled-back wallpaper and sticking the tape on top. Not the most seamless job, he wouldn't win any Christmas present wrapping tournaments, but hey. He relaxes, exhales, and smiles.

Silence.

"So… that's it?"

Tesla wags his eyebrows like *feces-is-insane-do-not-inquire*, so I don't, and we all just stare at the perfectly boring wallpaper for a minute. Then Aunt Barb slams her hand on the floor. "Well, waddya know? We're a team!" And she pulls Pete's earlobe.

Pete reaches up and holds her hand. "Wow, you always used to do that." And holy shit, Julie – his eyes start welling up. I walk over to them and look down. "Dude. With all the shi- *stuff* we've been through, I've never made you cry."

"Oh, trust me, you've made me cry. Many times. Just not in a good way."

"Whatever. So Nikola, let's pop back into the hallway and get us back to 2020 before Julie and Me-"

RRRRRIIIIIPPPPP.

Oh fuck. Did I just hear what I think I heard?

We look over together, I don't even know why because we already know the answer, and yeah, the rip in spacetime is back, twice as long and orangier and angrier than ever. No, this whatever-it-is is *not* going down that easy, with a little Aunt Barb tingle and two inches of scotch tape. I should've known.

"Not to worry, my friends. I had supposed our initial celebration might have been premature. This was expected."

"Well, since you say it like that, Nikola, I'm not so freaked out that entropy is collapsing and we're all going to die."

Gigi and Hannah look up at me. "Die?"

"No! No! I meant… *die-dee-doo*! We're all going to *die-dee-doo*! It's a, uh, dance! Come on everybody!"

And yeah, I get everyone up off the floor, in a desperate attempt to distract them from our imminent demise, and make up the *Die-Dee-Doo* dance on the fly.

How to Do the Die-Dee-Doo Dance (to Distract Your Children from Our Imminent Demise):

1. Stand up, form a circle, and wiggle your hips.
2. Wave your arms in the air like you just don't care. (Bobo made this part up.)
3. Step to the right.
4. Step to the left.
5. Step on each other's toes (this was an accident, but the kids thought this part was hilarious so I'm making it official).
6. Kick Chip in the shins really hard (Pete did this, because he's pissed at me for saying the word "die" in front of the kids, so of course Gigi and Hannah start pelting me with their cute little (but iron-toed) Timberlands, and even Aunt Barb and Tesla join in, boy everyone's just having a grand old time sending white hot bolts of pain through my poor shinbones, whatever, I deserve it).
7. Hold hands and turn clockwise and shout, "Die-Dee-Doo!"
8. Whisper-shout to Tesla, "Psst. Nikola. Please tell me you have a plan. All I've got is this dance."

So anyway, after we tucker the kids out a little (or actually, I'm tuckered out and the kids just get bored with the amazing Die-Dee-Doo Dance), Tesla nods to me, and us adults stand around his desk, looking down at him drawing incomprehensible lines and numbers. He looks around and realizes we're fucking morons, so he starts drawing stick figures instead.

"Chip and Pete. Do you remember the antimatter amplifier we used with Bill Montrose?"

"Who?"

"Bill Montrose."

"No, I know who you're talking about. Who."

"I am telling you who."

"No. WHO. The bad guy. The guy with the stupid name. Bill Montrose was his alternate, but a good guy version of WHO."

"Yes. Of course. Well, as Mister Montrose had a subtle ability to emit a trance-like field that we could amplify…" He draws another two stick figures and wavy lines… "I believe with a similar apparatus we could amplify the effect of Miss Barb and Master Pete's co-proximity."

Pete smiles. "Cool. So I have superpowers too? Like Chip?"

"I'm afraid, Pete, that it is not supernatural at all. You are just a normal human being."

"Just? Wow. Way to let me down easy, Nikola."

Tesla pats his arm and grins. "An exceptional human being, Pete. Perfect, my friend. But perfectly normal. As is Miss Barb. No, it is not yourselves that are exhibiting this power – it is your unique situation that is causing the strange healing behavior of the paradox tear." He doesn't even slow down, as our silence is his clue that we are, still and very much so, blank mental slates. "Let me explain:"

Nikola Tesla's Quickstart Guide to the Mystery of DNA and How to Use it to Control the Flow of Entropy
(wow that's a mouthful):

Step 1: Create a paradox. (Chip notes: do NOT do this on purpose. It's *very* bad. Tesla's just using it as a starting point. A simple way to create a paradox is to have two people from different points on the same timeline in the same dimension – say my wonderful daughter Gigi who never creates chaos, and the equally wonderful Nikola Tesla who also never creates chaos (I'm being sarcastic, of course, between the two of them my life is nothing *but* chaos) – anyway, have the two of them enter a single point on their home timeline and dimension. The resulting paradox will try to reconcile the contradiction by speeding up time to a point where the whole damn timeline collapses. Listen, if your brain hurts like mine trying to make sense of this, remember the ITA motto: *Shit's crazy. Don't ask.* Okay, I hand the mic back to Tesla.)

Step 2: Find direct relatives from the two different dates on the timeline. *This is the key*, and why my older apparition was trying to point us in the direction of Miss Barb. You see, the only two direct relatives from different dates in this room are she and Pete. The rest of us are either not related, or from the same date on the timeline. I believe the timeline, in its efforts to resolve the paradox, see Pete and Barb, because of their very close DNA structure, as essentially the same person, or close enough.

Step 3: Bring the two into proximity. By putting Miss Barb and Master Pete in contact and both in proximity to the paradox tear, we are signaling to it that it has already resolved the contradiction and collapsed the timeline. The person from the past has become, in a sense, the same person from the future, or again – close enough. Essentially we are tricking the paradox into believing it's already done its job.

Step 4: Supercoil their DNA chromosomes using radioactivity. (Pete interrupts here: "Woah. You're going to do what to my what using what?" It's my turn to snort, finally, but Pete punches me so hard it makes the snort not worth it.) Fear not, Master Pete. I believe we can construct a device that safely twists existing DNA strands using a radioactive isotope of say, polonium, those twists concentrating and amplifying the signal to the timeline. It will be an external device, Pete. A box with two compartments, one for you and one for Miss Barb. Like two coffins.

"Hold on. Like two *coffins*, dude?"

"Excuse me. Not the best analogy. Like two very small solitary-confinement prison cells."

"Oh, that's much better. I can't wait."

"Or perhaps a large freezer with enough room for two human bodies."

"Stop."

"I will put in windows."

"You know what, Nikola? Quit while you're behind. Whatever. What is this thing and how to we get it?"

Tesla waves his fingers a little, he can't help it, he does that sometimes when he's about to announce yet another of his incredible inventions, and the name for this one doesn't disappoint: "Ahem. We are about to construct the MULTIVERSE ENTROPY RESTABILIZING DNA ENERGIZER."

I think through the acronym for a second. "Uh, MERDE? Doesn't exactly roll off the tongue, Nikola."

"And we are naming things now so that they roll off the tongue?"

"I was hoping. This has to go into the book eventually, Nikola. MERDE, I don't know, just doesn't do anything for me."

Tesla's hand slams down on the desk. "Doesn't do anything for you? This device will save our-"

"Okay, okay! Forget it. Stop. MERDE it is. Whatever. Can I at least buy a fedora on the way out? I have a *one-pigeon-crapping-on-my-head-per-day* limit." I head for the hotel room door.

At that exact moment, the sun passes the building next to us, sending a ray of light onto Tesla's face, putting a glint in his eye. He picks up his INController. "Not *that* door, Chip. The INTERDIMENSIONAL TRANSFER APPARATUS. Our destination isn't New York."

"It's not?"

He grins. "No. Paris!"

Aunt Barb fans her face. *"Oh, gay Paree! Mon amour!* A dream of mine! I knew there was a reason I studied French in high school! Wait. Why are we going to Paris?"

"To see Marie Curie, of course."

7. I FINALLY WENT TO PARIS AND ALL I GOT WAS A FACE-EATING DINOSAUR.

From: Chip Collins
To: Julie Taylor
Date: February 29, 2020 8:19pm
Subject: I finally went to Paris and all I got was a face-eating dinosaur.

Hi Julie,

So this dinosaur is about to eat my face off, and I look down at Gigi, my last look at her, ever, shielding her from the inevitable, and I think, you know what? Maybe this is a better way for all of us to go, mauled by a velociraptor, versus the unknown, bottomless horror of the entire multiverse coming undone.

I know this is the worst possible time for a memory, but remember we took Gigi to that dino-park in Florida when we went to see your mom? It was that classic rundown Florida tourist trap experience, the poor plaster dinosaurs decaying and fading in the sun, herons making actual nests in the ones with weather-beaten, exposed innards. It was like an accidental recreation of the extinction of the dinosaurs, happening right now in slow motion, but this time the poor beasts were succumbing to the slow march of time and neglect rather than the quick knockout punch of a meteor. All I could think was, "Did we really just pay thirty bucks to get in here?"

"Wait, Chip. Look."

And I looked down and Gigi was petting the leg of a T-rex, staring straight up at its face in total awe. "Big Bobo."

"No honey, that's not a Bobo. That's a Tyrannosaurus Rex."

"Tyra!"

"Yeah. I guess. Like Tyra Banks. Sure. She your girlfriend?"

Gigi nodded and did her little jig. "Tyra! Fren!" And so we climbed the rickety *held-together-with-rust* ladder so Gigi could sit on her new friend's back and pretend to ride her like a pony (while you and me wondered which we would die from: A) this flimsy contraption collapsing under the weight of three people, or B) the tetanus we were all going to get after we cut ourselves on one of the million sharp rusty edges).

We didn't die, and in fact we had a blast, and it was Gigi's favorite thing ever, and I realized, once again, why tourist traps should continue to exist, despite all their kitsch and disregard for safety and sanitation: because they give you something to remember, another memory to smile at or roll your eyes at or laugh about when you're old and gray. That shit is the bomb.

Fuck. Where was I? Oh yeah. About to have my face eaten off. So I peer back up from Gigi into the dinosaur's eyes, it soulless, menacing eyes, and I can hear Gigi calling out "Tyra! Tyra! Fren!" and I'm thinking "oh baby, I'm sorry to say this but you are so very wrong," and the thing snaps its claw at my face and opens its maw, here comes lunch, and I close my eyes and clutch Gigi and wait for death, and I hear:

"Tyra? Do I look like a Tyra?"

I open one eye. *Who said that?*

"Ahem. Do I look like a Tyra?"

Holy fuck.

A talking dinosaur.

Wait. Whoops. You're asking "How the hell did you get from 'Let's go to Paris' to a talking dinosaur?" (Btw, we're not talking about Barney the talking dinosaur. We're talking about Barney's exact scary-as-shit opposite, but more on that later.) I know, by now I should be better at keeping you up to speed, it's been three books already for Christ's sake, I shouldn't have to rely on flashbacks to get you back to the present. Sorry. Just one more wee little flashback. I promise. Never again. I know, never say never, but trust me. Yeah, okay, forget I said trust me. Whatever. It's flashback time.

So Tesla proclaims, "On to Paris!" scribbles a few notes into his journal, and Barb is practically tearing a hole through the ITA door to start her adventure, and I'm like "Uh, don't you think seven people's kind of a lot, well, six people and Bobo, but it's a lot, right? We should leave the kids here with Barb."

"Excellent idea, Master Chip."

But Gigi and Hannah aren't thinking this I such an excellent idea. They both plod over to me and pull my shirt so I lean down close. Gigi whispers, "I not see Mommy too?"

"No. No. I'm not going to see Mommy. I'm going to find some stuff, to build a thing, to make the bad orange sesame chicken thing go away, so we can both go see Mommy."

"We stay alone?"

Damn. I know where this is going. "No, no, honey. Great Aunt Barb is going to stay with you."

Gigi nods, but her eyes are getting wet, and she's starting to sniff. Oh man, she's trying to be a good girl, trying so hard to be brave, but now her whole body's shaking, hers and Hannah's both.

It's no use. I fold like a cheap lawn chair. "Fuck it. They're coming with us."

"Chip! Language!"

"Berries, okay? Berries, they're coming with us."

Gigi and Hannah squeal through their tears and jump into my arms. And I get it: we're all we've got, this little family of ours. We might be all that's left of 2020. We might not have a home to come home to. So for now, we're each other's home. I squeeze them a little tighter. "Okay. You're coming with us. But Aunt Barb's your point person, got it? Like Mary Poppins, like your magic nanny. Okay?"

They both nod again, and look up at Barb. She whips out a hankie from her Mary Poppins bag and dabs their eyes dry. "There. Good as new. Now before we head out, girlfriends, I've got a little something for you." She reaches once more into her purse and pulls out something hidden in her hands. Then she puts her fingers behind the girls' ears and pulls them out, revealing two quarters. The girls are amazed, I don't think they've ever seen the old *quarters-from-behind-your-ears* trick, and they clap like she's an even better magician than Tesla. Barb slips the quarters into that little extra pocket in their jeans (Hey! *That's* what that tiny pocket's for! Quarters!), and she whispers, "Now don't spend it all on handsome boys," and pulls their earlobes.

Well. If we die in the past and collapse this whole thing, at least we landed the most kick-ass babysitter in the multiverse. Barb rocks. Pete pats me on the back. "Good call, dude."

Barb turns to us, holding Gigi and Hannah's hands, even more excited now that she gets to go on an adventure *and* play Mary Poppins. "Okie-dokey, gents. Lead on!"

So we're walking, and walking, and walking, you know how it is in here, I can't tell if we're walking for ten minutes or five hours, all of us pretty quiet, with a mix of hope and excitement and fear and dread, and after a while I see Aunt Barb tug Pete's shirt and say low, "So… I never got married?"

"No. You used to tell me it would get in the way of all the romance."

She grins. "Oooh. Tell me more."

"Apparently you were quite the catch. Lots of suitors. You would joke and say they were all Mister Right. They just weren't Mister *The One*. The last boyfriend I remember, and you were in your seventies at the time, he was a cowboy. A real-life, ten-gallon-hat, cattle-wrangling, good-ol' boy from Montana. Easily twenty years younger than you. I don't know how the hell he wound up in Brooklyn, I think you said he saw a picture of you on AOL and rode a horse all the way here to meet you."

She laughs. "That's just like something I'd say. What's AOL?"

"The early days of the Internet."

"What's the Internet?"

"Oh boy."

They walk a little while longer, quiet, then she asks, "So, what happened to the cowboy? He sounded perfect."

"You said you ditched him because he smoked too much."

"Ha!" She digs into her bag for a cigarette and lights up. "Smokes too much? For me?"

"Yeah. He was like a three-pack-a-day-er, Mom wouldn't even let him in the house."

"Your mom. She'd be my… niece. Gosh, that's weird."

I stride up to them. "You know what's weird?"

Pete looks around. "Everything?"

"Well, yeah. Of course. But also – once we get to this other dimension, how the hell are we getting to Paris? You know how long it takes to fly a plane, or sail a boat, over there? It's the whole Pacific Ocean."

"It's the Atlantic Ocean, dude."

"Whatever. I'm thinking we don't have that kind of time."

Tesla turns his head to us, still walking in the lead, smiling that inventor smile of his, that smile he has when he knows something special and can't wait to share it. But he doesn't say anything.

Barb puts out her cigarette with her heel and Bobo, walking behind us, picks it up and pops it in his mouth. I mean, come on, Bobo. Do you like the taste? Are you eating them, or saving them for later or something? Do Pall Malls have some kind of nutritional value I'm not aware of? Or are you helping clean up the multiverse up one cigarette butt at a time?

Tesla interrupts my really important train of thought with that sneaky smile again. I jog up to him. "Okay, Nikola. The suspense is killing me. How do we get all the way to Paris?"

He stops, looks down at the INController, takes a few more steps to the next door, and hands the INController to Bobo. "Ahem. As you know, young sirs, I have been traveling the INTERDIMENSIONAL TRANSFER APPARATUS for a very long time. There are many ways to travel great distances."

And with the deft hand of someone who's done this a zillion times, Tesla dials in zero-zero-zero-zero on the latch and pulls open the door with its familiar whoosh.

"Wow."

Through the doorway the sun is setting, and we're in the middle of a forest – except we're three stories up, floating above the tree line, so we can see pretty far into the distance, the lights of a city. It's beautiful. Wait. There it is. "The Eiffel Tower."

"Yes, Master Chip."

"But… how?"

"This dimension – and remember, there are infinite possibilities, Chip – has two advantageous qualities: first, the rotation of Earth in this dimension is ever-so-slightly slower. So when the INTERDIMENSIONAL TRANSFER APPARATUS was first formed here, instead of appearing in New York, it appeared in the Domaniale Forest just outside of Paris."

"Cool." I look at the ground, guessing about 30 feet below us. And sniff the air. Uh oh. That familiar aroma. Coming from either Gigi or Hannah. "Odor alert. How do we get down?"

"I wasn't finished, Chip. Don't you want to know the second advantageous quality of this dimension?"

"Sure. But please tell me it has something to do with unlimited free diapers, because my nose is telling me one of these angels is going to explode in t-minus two minutes. And that's not negotiable."

Tesla ignores me. (And apparently the smell. Amazing.) "Ahem. The second advantageous quality of this dimension is that Marie Curie, unlike in our home dimension, is still alive! And with her superior knowledge of radioisotopes, she should be able to help us with the construction of the MULTIVERSE ENTROPY RESTABILIZING DNA ENERGIZER."

"Cool. Great. Okay, *now* how do we get down? I'm not kidding, Nikola. This hallway's about to get so toxic we might have to jump."

Tesla goes to check his watch in his vest pocket, but realizes it's not there. I reach into my jeans and take it out, the old stopwatch he gave me after the Blue Juice Missile Crisis, I never leave home without it, always keep it perfectly timed, his sweet reminder to me that I should evermore look forward. I turn it over a couple of times, then place it in Tesla's palm. "It's ironic, Nikola. You gave me this with a message to always look forward, and here we are, looking back to 1947 for answers."

He admires his watch, smiling. "1945."

"1947. Come on, Nikola. I'm just getting the hang of this. It's 1947. Don't throw me off."

"All right. Then I won't tell you that because of this dimension's slightly slower Earth rotation, each day, week, month, and year is slightly longer relative to our own, and that we are peering into what they consider 1945. The month of May, I believe."

"Yeah. Good. Don't tell me that. Just tell me how we get down. My eyes are starting to sting."

Tesla grins again, that grin, and points down. Maybe a hundred yards away, something's rumbling through the brush, snapping branches, tearing this way like a bat out of (or maybe into) hell.

"Mon amie! Mon amie! I am sorry to be late!"

A candy-apple-red roadster convertible blasts out into the little clearing below us, dragging plants and shit, leaving two-inch deep skid marks in the dirt, squirrels are leaping out of the way for dear life, and behind the wheel is an old French woman with big black goggles, laughing, waving a journal. Huh. They told me Marie Curie was a Nobel-Prize-winning physicist and chemist, but she looks like a professional rally car driver to me.

And those funky goggles. Big black orbs. They remind me of someone. I turn to Bobo. "Hey buddy, look. One of your own."

"BEEZNEEZ."

So the old lady screeches to a stop right under us, dusts off her dress, goes to the trunk and pulls out a crossbow.

I swear to God, every time I think I've seen the strangest shit, something like this happens. Marie Curie, Nobel-Prize-winning physicist and chemist, has gone insane and is about to fucking kill us with a crossbow. Yeah. I think this one takes the cake.

Oh. Wait. There's a rope attached to the end of the arrow.

Schwing!

"Bouge de lá! Get out of ze way!" (She screams this *after* the arrow comes hurtling dangerously close to my face, instead of *before.* Gee thanks, Marie!)

Okay, long story every-so-slightly-less-long, the ass-end of this rope is a ladder, so we fasten it down good, shimmy down, me and Pete carrying the diaper-grenades (I mean our precious daughters), and the second I hit the ground I rush over to Madame Curie, no introductions, and hold Gigi up to her nose, and I don't even have to say the word "diapers" in French (which I couldn't do anyway because I don't know a single word of French other than "oui") and she scrambles over to the trunk, rummaging around, and shouts, "Violá!"

No, it's not disposables, or even diapers at all.

It's a Nazi flag.

She tears it right down the middle and hands the pieces to Barb, along with a smile. Barb curtsies, a little in awe, and says, "Merci. Ravi de vous rencontrer."

"Ah! You speak French! Yes, you are very welcome, and it ees a pleasure to meet you too!"

I shake her hand. "Hello Madame Curie. Chip Collins. Um, why you have a Nazi flag in your trunk?"

"'Twas for later. For ze burning. But I sink zis is an even more appropriate end for zat evil sing, no?" She laughs.

I watch Barb going to work like a ninja diaper changer. "Nazi flag burning? Am I missing something, Nikola?"

Tesla looks down at his watch again. "I was right. May, 1945. You aren't missing anything, Master Chip. On the contrary, I believe we are just in time." He walks over to Madame Curie and they exchange a bone-crushing embrace, and Tesla leans down and whispers in her ear, "Marie. It is so very nice to see you again. But I'm afraid there is no time to celebrate. We need your help."

She scoffs at him playfully. "I will help, of course, my dear friend. But… zere is always time to celebrate!"

So we stuff ourselves into her race car and speed off toward Paris.

As we get closer to the Champs-Élysées, we slow to a crawl. There are people everywhere, clogging every street, parading around, singing, popping champagne bottles, waving at us. Gigi and Hannah are waving back. It's obviously a parade for them, right? Wait… I was being sarcastic, but… maybe it is a parade for them?

"Hey, Nikola. Is this for us? Like, did all these people know you were coming?"

Shaking his head and smiling, Tesla points to our right. People waving French, American, and British flags, and a nearby bin containing what I assume is a Nazi flag ablaze and turning to ash.

Suddenly two fighter planes buzz right over our heads, insanely loud, dropping flares into the street, and way down the end of the avenue, fireworks explode over the Arc de Triomphe.

Yes, Julie, it took all this for me to realize: "World War Two?"

Madame Curie nods and smiles the happiest smile I may ever have seen, waving to all the people she's nearly plowing down with her car. "Yes, Chip. May 9, 1945. The Nazis have surrendered. Peace is ours. It is Victory Day!"

We pass a band playing the U.S. national anthem, and Julie, I gotta say: I have never been more proud to be an American. We're actually *here*, at the exact moment we defeated the bad guys, the moment we won, the moment the forces for good worked together and peace prevailed in the world. I look over at Pete, and he says, "Wow, this is awesome," and when I lean across he's like, "But it's still not hug time." Oh well.

Some random person hands me a bottle of champagne. "Lève un verre à l'avenir!"

Aunt Barb pats my knee. "I think he said, 'Raise a glass to the future!'"

And so I raise the bottle, and take a swig, and feel the rush of victory, and peace, and the hope of the future. This *rocks*.

Wait. The future.

I think about the orange tear in the fabric of the multiverse.

I watch Gigi and Hannah giggle and dance for their fans, oblivious and giddy with little kid joy.

I watch Aunt Barb taking pictures (wait, she's got a *camera* in that bag too?) and doing her best Queen Elizabeth wave to her subjects. She is having the time of her life.

I look at Pete, dousing himself and Tesla in champagne, both of them laughing like teenagers.

And finally, I look down at Bobo, and I don't know why, he never answers me, but I ask him, "How does it end?"

And he gives me the finger.

Thanks, Bobo.

8. WHOOPS. THIS IS THE PART ABOUT THE FACE-EATING DINOSAUR.

From: Chip Collins
To: Julie Taylor
Date: February 29, 2020 8:19pm
Subject: Whoops. This is the part about the face-eating dinosaur.

Hi Julie,

Okay, I'm getting to the dinosaur.

So we're in Marie Curie's lab now (I had imagined it would be directly beneath the Eiffel Tower, her vast underground lair like twenty stories down, complete with the Avengers quinjet and a nuclear reactor, but no, it's just some random three-room laboratory on the sixth floor of some random building on some random Paris street. Some random guy Calvin even had to buzz us up.) After a nice, long, well-deserved nap, we're invited over into the lab part, and I spot something weird out of the corner of my eye. Something's peeking out from behind a cabinet.

"What the fuck is that? Excuse my French."

"Zat is French? What French is zat?"

"Forget it. What the- what the-"

But before I can let loose another French swearword, it's coming at us, straight for me and Gigi.

A fucking dinosaur!

Seven feet tall, a velociraptor I think (look at me, Chip the Paleontologist), with razor-sharp claws, an escapee from Jurassic Park, moving on us like the professional hunter it is, and for just a split-second – the last split-second I have left in my short life – I wonder why no one else is screaming like a little girl, not even the two little girls right next to me.

And that's when the near-death moment happens, and Gigi squeals "Tyra!" and the thing says, calm as anything, "Tyra? Do I look like a Tyra?"

I'm gobsmacked. (Wow, I got to use that word twice. (Btw, don't be surprised if you see it again.)) "What the *fuck?!* Excuse my French again."

"Master Chip!"

Marie shouts, "Zat is not French!"

And the dinosaur (not big purple cuddly Barney, not by a fucking long shot) rolls its eyes, like it's been in this predicament many, many times before, and sighs. "My name is Calvin. All right, let's get this over with. You newbies are all the same. How far back shall I go? To when the Earth cooled?"

"Why am I the only one freaking out about this?!"

I whip my head around, and everyone just kind of shrugs. Pete says, "Dude. Marie told us on the way here. You were too busy talking to Bobo."

"BEEZNEEZ."

"Okay, whatever. Yeah, 'shit's crazy don't ask,' I get it. But man, Tyr- Calvin, you just scared the piss out of me and my kid." I point down to Gigi, who's already hugging his leg. "Okay. Well, you scared the piss out of *me*. Whatever. Can somebody catch me up?"

And Calvin cracks his knuckles and inhales, and I crack my own knuckles and take out my phone, because here comes another mini-sub-novel:

SHITSTORM: The Adventures of Calvin the Dinosaur, Nazi Spy Ninja
(As told by Calvin the Dinosaur, ghost-written by Chip (Master-of-Interdimensional-Travel) Collins)

Calvin throws his snout up in the air. "The *dinosaur*? Really? That's like titling your story *Chip the Mammal*. If you're going to be childish, at least be specific. Calvin the *Deinonychus*. And ninja? You're just making things up."

"Sorry, it sounded cool. Ninja makes everything sound cool. I'll take it out in the second draft. Hey, is deinonychus the same as velociraptor?"

"Do I look like a velociraptor?"

I fidget. "Yes…?"

"And the title: *Shitstorm*. Any bearing on reality? At all?"

I shrug. "Sounds… cool?"

He just rolls his eyes and begins the unbelievable tale…

"Ahem. In our dimension, the meteor extinction event, approximately sixty-six million years ago, didn't quite do the trick. A tiny number of our species survived – no other species, including velociraptor, escaped death – and we scattered across the globe, isolated, alone, hiding in small groups, biding our time, like the beings you call Sasquatch or Bigfoot."

I jump to my feet. "Wait! Are they real? Bigfoots?"

"Intelligent Deinonychi living in secret isolation for millennia, it makes perfect sense. But Bigfoots? Come, Mister Collins – don't be ridiculous." And he actually physically pushes me back down into my chair and continues.

"In 1923, Madame Marie Curie was on a research expedition in Russia, and found me, bleeding and barely alive in a bear trap. She exclaimed, 'Mon Dieu! Cette pauvre créature!,' and saved me from death."

Marie chimes in, "He was so brave, not a single tear, with a smile even on his face."

Calvin gives her a polite little nod, though I catch a little eye-roll in there. "Ah, yes, Marie. In any event, we spoke at length, and-"

I raise my hand, ever the good student. "Um. Sorry. Question. You knew French?"

"Ah. I keep forgetting. You are ignorant. You see, we Deinonychi do not have enormous brains, but they are *extremely* dense with neurons, making us – obviously – much smarter than most humans. How do you think we were able to evade discovery for millions of years?"

"Hold on. If you're so smart, why didn't you evolve and build cities and take over, instead of humans?"

His eyes flicker. Is that rage? Maybe he's just constipated. "There are things, Mister Collins, I'm afraid you wouldn't understand. Including the fact that we can learn languages like French in mere moments. Moving on: Marie smuggled me here, to Paris, under absolute secrecy, and began teaching me about radioactivity, and soon I was helping her with her experiments."

Marie crosses to him and pats his arm. "Calvin here helped me win ze Nobel in 1911, though I couldn't give him credit, of course."

"I'm not bitter."

"I didn't say you were bitter, my son."

"Please don't call me that in front of guests, Marie."

"Gee, I'm not catching even the slightest whiff of bitterness in there, Calvin."

"Kindly shut up, Mister Collins." Calvin's death claw taps

impatiently on the tile floor. "May I continue?"

I shudder. This guy creeps me out. But he takes my involuntary body shake as a yes and moves on:

"In 1933, as I believe happened in your dimension as well, Hitler was named Chancellor of Germany, and immediately began his explorations into the occult, and conspiracy theories, one of which, of course, was our existence. He managed to find and capture a clutch of seven Deinonychi, corralling them into a prison laboratory, forcing them to learn as much as possible about nuclear energy. They were given numbers, not even names, and tasked with singular goal."

"The atomic bomb."

"Yes, Mister Collins. Perhaps you're not as cretinous as you look."

I smile. I mean, I know it was an insult wrapped in a compliment, but whatever. I'll take it.

"Marie and I found out, of course, as our contributions to the study of radiation were instrumental to their research. She tried to bring her discovery to the authorities, but at that time, before the war, there was no reason to believe any nefarious actions by the Germans were afoot. And so nothing was done. We were forced to…" he stops, looking down, and Marie continues for him.

"We allowed poor Calvin to be found and captured, to act as a spy." She puts her arms around him. "And to sabotage the program."

Calvin physically winces. Damn, this is rough stuff. "Dude. I'm sorry."

He waves me off and continues. "The program, titled Operation Dino Kaboom-"

"Woah. Hold on. You said I was childish for calling you a dinosaur, and these guys call their top-secret atomic bomb program *Operation Dino Kaboom?*"

"They were worse than childish. They were ignorant and stupid and evil. We were tortured. Barely fed. Worked until our brains couldn't think. And still they pushed.

"I slowly revealed to the seven my true identity, secretly, as we had developed a language of clicks and body movements in order to speak freely among the Nazis. And so, in the months that followed, we developed a bomb. But not the bomb they were asking for."

"Wait. Let me guess. And you dug a tunnel out of the dungeon lab, and blew the place to smithereens."

Calvin looks gobsmacked (that's number three). "How- How did you know that?"

Pete finally pipes up. "He does that sometimes. Uses his brain. Makes a good guess out of nowhere."

"Hey! I use my brain all the time, dude."

"If you say so."

Calvin harrumphs, I mean I've stolen his thunder a little, telling the climax of his story, but he's determined to get it back. "I cannot tell you, standing there outside the compound, watching the shitstorm – *Ah! You were right about the title after all, Mister Collins!* – watching the shitstorm unfold before us, as Nazis fled in all directions, and flames devoured everything around us. It was the first time I had seen destruction on such a scale. There is nothing like it, watching something burn like that. *Kaboom,* indeed."

His eyes are dancing in his head, like a crazy man, reliving it. Then he exhales, and looks around at us. "It was terrible. But we survived, the eight of us, and disappeared, to the far corners of the globe. The bomb program was gone. The Nazis began to falter. And ultimately," he looks out the window, "we won."

Gigi walks over to him and hugs his leg. "Thanks Tyra."

"Why does the child insist on calling me Tyra?"

"See, we took her to this dinosaur park in Flori- never mind. Dude, that's some dark stuff. But man, you saved everybody in this dimension from a pretty bleak future. You saved them from the end."

He looks wistfully at me. "I did, didn't I?"

9. RUE DANTON, PARIS, 1945

From: Chip Collins
To: Julie Taylor
Date: February 29, 2020 8:19pm
Subject: Rue Danton, Paris, 1945

Hi Julie,

"Has Nikola ever told you what a good dancer he is?"

Marie is chuckling to herself, nudging Tesla with her elbow. We're standing around her huge lab table, looking at a blueprint of some mixture of a spaceship and a torture device, man this is some serious stuff, and thank God, Marie's trying to keep it light. "He would make my late husband Pierre so jealous!"

I nudge Tesla too. "So, you doing a little Charleston, huh?"

"No. That was much later. In the early 1900s Marie and I would dance the Grizzly Bear, and the Turkey Trot, and the Bunny Hug."

"Animal dances. Cool. Were they as cool as the Die-Dee-Doo Dance?"

"Die-Dee-Doo! Die-Dee-Doo!" And yeah, you guessed it, Gigi and Hannah make us all do the Die-Dee-Doo Dance again, and wow, I never thought my shins could hurt this much from all the damn kicking. We let the kids and Bobo continue on their own (they'll have to decide which one of them gets kicked in the shins), and we get back to the table. (Not that I'll be doing anything but nodding and harrumphing.)

Marie points to the little box between the two coffins and shakes her head. "No, not polonium. Not powerful enough. I'm sorry, Nikola."

Tesla suddenly looks shaken. "Then, this entire journey…?"

Marie chuckles and pulls on some serious-looking leather gloves. Opening a small refrigerator behind her, she uses tongs to lift out a small tube, placing it reverently in the middle of the table. Inside the tube, if you look close, is another teeny tube, with a few drops of clear liquid inside. She winks at Tesla. "No, no, my dear Nikola, your journey was not in vain. In order to power ze MULTIVERSE ENTROPY RESTABILIZING DNA ENERGIZER, you'll need zis."

I bend down and peer into the vial. "Eye drops?"

She laughs. "Ah! Chip, I don't sink you want to use zis in your eyes! It's radium."

"Radium? Is that like rhodium? Like the metal the INController is made out of? And BOK's horn?"

"Who is BOK?"

"How much time do you have?"

She considers it, but I can see she knows I'll take three hours to tell her the story of BOK and the legend of *The Demon and the King*, and she decides to move on. "No, Chip, *rhodium* is a noble metal, like platinum, though even more rare. *Radium* is what we need: a radioactive element one million times more radioactive than uranium. My late husband and I discovered it. The decay of just one drop of this should have just the right frequency, ah, 'good tone' if you will. *Bon ton.*"

"BONTON. BONTON."

"Ah! Our leettle friend Bobo here speaks!"

I hunt around for a paperclip. "Marie, don't encourage him." But the leg humping has already started, and she's kind of getting a kick out of it.

"BONTON. BONTON."

"My! You are a feisty leettle sing!"

"He'll be done in a minute."

Pete raises his hand. "Um, listen. I'm hearing 'a million times more radioactive than uranium' and 'Pete's DNA' used in the same sentence. Am I going to grow three heads or something?"

Marie smacks his hand playfully. "Nonsense! No, ze radium will be housed like zis, in a double shield, and will only interact with DNA taken from a few hairs from each of you. It will simply be amplifying ze effect zat your bodies, in co-proximity but a safe distance from ze radium, are having on ze paradox." She waves her arms at all of us. "Now. All of you but Nikola and Calvin. Class time is over. Leave us. Ze grownups have to get to work."

"Did you say grownups? That's my cue!" And I grab the kids and me and Pete and Barb head for the door. Calvin shoos Bobo out with us too (and believe me, you don't say no to a seven-foot-tall deinonychus), and we all leave them to craft whatever mad-scientist-mind-bending doohickey they're cooking up.

Out on the street, the kids are waving at all their new French friends, the whole vibe is still very celebratory, I mean we just won a world war, right? I notice on the corner a little hubbub (not quite a commotion - hey, see what I did there, I got to use two of my favorite words at once, "hubbub" *and* "commotion"), anyway there are people surrounding one of those statue-people performers. This one looks like a Roman centurion. Cool.

Wait. The guy's not standing still. He's scared. Looking around, like "where the fuck am I?" waving his hands around for the people to stay away from him, but they're clapping and shit, it's all part of the act, right?

No. It isn't. The guy's scared because he's an *actual Roman centurion*. Another one of those temporal anomalies. What the hell is going on?

"Hey, Pete, look at thi-" but he's gone. They're up ahead at the gelato place. But I can't take my eyes off this centurion guy to catch up to them. I'm glued to the spot.

A voice to my left. "Weird, right?"

I whip around. Look down. A teenage girl points her chin at the hubbub. Looks up at me and grins.

Huh. There's something about her face. Something.

Oh my God.

"Gigi?"

"Hey Dad."

"Oh my God, Gigi!" I pick her up and twirl her around. She's practically weightless. "Is it really you?"

"Good question. This is equally weird for me. I'm not from around here. Where are we?"

"Paris. 1945. I think you're a temporal anomaly."

"Temporal anomaly? Pretty fancy words for you, Dad."

My eyes well up. "You know me. Fancy word guy." God, I can't believe I'm having a conversation with our teenage daughter. She was two years old a minute ago. "Hey, honey, why are you here? Or is it just random, like that centurion?"

"No, I think I'm here because I have a question."

I lean down to get a close look. Yes, same eyes, just older, maybe fourteen or so, same dimples, same reddish brown hair, that perfect mix of Julie and Chip hair. "Sure, Gigi. What's up?"

"What was Mom like?"

It's like a punch in the stomach.

. . .

This anomaly, I don't know, does she represent some possibility of a future where we never get back to 2020? Where our baby girl never gets to know you? My heart starts hurting, breaking into pieces, I can hardly stand it. I'm wiping back the tears now. "Well, you know what the Old Man would say."

She laughs, a light little laugh, from somewhere far away. "Yeah. He'd say she was the bee's knees."

"The bee's knees. She was. But God, she was – *is* – so much more. When she smiles, it's like the glow from a campfire, it warms you and keeps you safe from the dark. Like your smile. Actually, exactly like your smile. And she had this way of burping you, it was hilarious. She'd swish you back and forth across her chest, then suddenly bring you up to her shoulder, and you'd burp, and she would shower you with kisses. And then you got a little older, so you didn't need burping, but you'd still climb into bed sometimes and crawl onto her and squeal "bup!" just to get the swish and the kisses all over. Oh, there's so much more I need to tell yo-"

But I can't even get the words out. I'm heaving, sobbing, it's hard to breathe. I'm bent over, on my knees now, lost.

She pats my back. Yes, once again, our daughter is comforting her blubbering dad. I'm pathetic.

Then, I don't know why, I burp.

We both laugh. "That's better, Dad." She kisses me on the head. "Well look at me. Just like Mom."

I raise my head, enough so we're eye-to-eye. And I realize. It's Gigi. But it's also you in there. I can see you. Through time and space and dimensions. God, I could stay here forever. But I can't. "Julie. We're coming to get you."

Her smile fades, and she kisses me on the cheek one last time. "I know. But you better get your ass in gear."

And I'm left there, on the sidewalk of Rue Danton, in Paris of 1945, talking to thin air, on my knees.

I don't notice the group of women veering to avoid me, or the guy taking a coin from his pocket and tossing it at my feet. All I notice are my hands shaking, and a thought pounding against my skull, over and over:

Time is running out.

From: Chip Collins
To: Julie Taylor
Date: February 29, 2020 8:19pm
Subject: Re: Rue Danton, Paris, 1945

Hi Julie,

I feel someone kneel down next to me. "Is this some kind of performance art thing?"

"Oh. Hey, Pete. Aren't you with the girls?"

"Barb's finishing up with their ice cream. I think they got more on their clothes than in their mouths. I saw you over here looking like Hobo Doomsday Preacher and figured I'd come save you. You okay?"

"Dude, I just had the weirdest experience."

"Define weirdest. I'm thinking we've done a lot of weirdests."

I get up onto my feet, pocketing the change I've been accumulating, and pick him up. "Well first I saw that centurion…" I look back to where he was, but he's gone. "… Well, he was there a minute ago. Then I met Gigi. But she was older. But it was Julie too. Dude, shit's getting more weird than usual, and I feel like time is definitely not our friend right now."

"Hey. Don't worry. By tomorrow morning they'll have my little prison cell thing built, and we'll be on our way back to normal."

I laugh. "Back to normal. I don't know. Do we ever get that back?"

"We'll get back boys. You betcha." Sauntering over to us is Barb, who's pretending to be oblivious to the whistles of various Parisian gentlemen. She lights up a cigarette and hands the pack to Pete.

"I know, I know. I'm a bad influence. But you boys look like you could use one."

Pete pulls one out and lights it, and as usual, looks like he was born for this. I, on the other hand, start hacking up half of one of my lungs, and spitting uncontrollably. "Not the smoker I was in ninth grade anymore I guess. Hey Barb, I'm scared to ask, but where are the girls and Bobo?"

"Oh, they started chanting about seeing Old Man, and well…"

"Yeah, it's over when they start doing that."

"Bingo. But Nikola was happy to see them. I think he needed a break."

A kitten, from nowhere, starts zig-zagging through our legs slowly, purring. I go down to pet it, and it runs away. But then it stops and looks back. It wants to play. So we follow it a little, this playful little thing, and suddenly it dashes into a gutter hole and disappears.

"Cute." I bend down and look into the hole. Nothing.

And as I'm coming up, I notice it.

The latch on the door to the office building right in front of me.

A latch with a luggage lock.

The door. That gray. That lock. It's exactly like a door in the ITA. No, not like.

It is that lock.

"Pete. You seeing this?"

"Yup. Step away, dude."

So me and Pete back up a few paces, staring, but Barb approaches it.

"Barb. That's a bad thing. A very bad thing. Let's go upstairs and tell Tesla."

"Oh, come on now, fellas. Where's your sense of adventure?"

Pete laughs. "It left us the second we stepped into the ITA for the first time. Adventure's overrated."

"Well, I think it behooves us to peek inside. It could be nothing. We don't want to alarm Nikola unnecessarily."

Pete turns to me. "It behooves us. Great. She's starting to sound like you."

I'm just staring at the lock. "No. I don't like this, Barb. God knows where that door leads. Give me one good reason we should try it."

In answer, she points up to the brass numbers above the transom.

2020. Of course.

"It's a coincidence, Barb. Come on, let's go ups-"

But before the words leave my mouth, before we can grab her, she's flipping the zeros, turning the latch and jumping in.

10. AND YOU THOUGHT TALKING DINOSAURS WAS WEIRD.

From: Chip Collins
To: Julie Taylor
Date: February 29, 2020 8:19pm
Subject: And you thought talking dinosaurs was weird.

Hi Julie,

Dammit!

Barb's gone! Barb is the key!

Oh wait. There she is. Way off in the distance down this dirt road we're on.

"Hey, is that your Great Aunt Barb being kidnapped by some dude in armor on the back of a unicorn?"

"I never thought I'd hear you say that, but yes."

"Well it's a good thing it's not real." I look around at the low stone buildings, the old wooden pull carts, the smell, obviously not 2020, or even 1945. "It's just a temporal anomaly."

"It seems pretty fucking real to me." Pete pulls his foot out of a big pile of unicorn shit.

"Right. I guess real or not we're going to have to save her." I instinctively check my phone to see if there's an Uber around. Nope. Not here in whatever-the-fuck year we're in. "Gotta catch up to them. Where the hell are we going to get a couple of unicorns? We need bait."

"We're not fishing, dude."

"Yeah, we're fishing for unicorns. I think it's virgins. Something about unicorns and virgins."

"Don't look at me."

I start turning around, screaming in all directions. "Come here virgins! Or unicorns! Actually unicorns is what we really need! But we'll take a virgin if it'll get us a unicorn!"

"Stop. Please. And by the way, why would you think they'd call them unicorns in this dimension? They probably call them horn horses. That's all they are. Horses with horns. Horn horses."

"Wow. You've got a lot to learn, dude. Not anywhere, in any dimension, in all of infinity, would they call that majestic creature a horn horse. That's blasphemy. They're called unicorns. Beautiful word for a beautiful, magical animal."

"Whatever. You can shut up now. Let's just ask this lady."

And sure enough, there's a woman trotting down the road, on, you guessed it: a unicorn.

"Excuse me, ma'am! We need help."

She looks down from her mount suspiciously. "Qui diable êtes-vous?"

Fuck. French. Of course.

But Pete's on the case. "Oh, hey, my phone. I've got that Google translate thing. I don't think I need Internet for it. Lemme try." He pulls it out and types "We need your help" and it actually speaks it in French! The woman is gobsmacked (that's four times now if you're keeping track), gaping at Pete's magic rectangle, she's just this side of calling the local high priest to have us drawn-and-quartered in the square for witchcraft, but her curiosity gets the better of her. "D'où êtes-vous?"

Man, this app rocks. It translates her spoken words to English. Pete reads his screen. "She wants to know where we're from."

I clear my throat. "Greetings. We're from Paris. On Earth."

She throws her head back and cackles. "Tout le monde est de la terre imbécile! Et nous sommes à Paris, putain de merde!"

"Pete, what? What did she say?"

"She said, 'Everyone's from Earth you idiots. And we're *in* Paris, dumbfuck.'"

She's pointing in the direction the armor dude absconded (another favorite word, btw) with Barb, and yup, there it is, way off in the distance, three-quarters completed: Notre Dame cathedral. "Okay, confirmed. We're in medieval France."

"Yeah. *Now* you can ask me for a shilling."

I walk over to the woman, she's calming down a bit, enjoying us two court jesters. She's so relaxed she's taken out a needle and thread and is darning her pantaloons. Distracted much?

"Ahem. Excuse me. Ma'am. Wouldn't want to interrupt your nifty needlework there, but might we borrow your unicorn?"

"Qu'est-ce qu'une 'unicorn'?"

"She's asking what's a unicorn."

I point to her unicorn.

She cackles again. "Ce? c'est mon cheval de corne."

Pete's cackling now. He doesn't even have to say it, he just walks over and shows me the phone screen and it says, "This? It's my horn horse."

From: Chip Collins
To: Julie Taylor
Date: February 29, 2020 8:19pm
Subject: Re: And you thought talking dinosaurs was weird.

Hi Julie,

So we talk the lady into letting us borrow her unicor– I mean horn horse – by giving her one of my "enchanted squares." Yeah, it's just my Starbucks rewards card, but we told her it made delicious hot beverages appear out of nowhere. (Which is actually true, if you buy ten coffees first, and I think I'm due, so all she has to do is find the nearest medieval Starbucks and she's golden.)

Now we're trotting towards Notre Dame on her unic– fuck, *horn horse* – and let me tell you, I've only ridden a horse once or twice in my life, but I don't remember it sucking so bad, like I don't know, you expect riding a uni– fuck it, no I'm not correcting myself anymore, it's a goddam *unicorn*, anyway you'd expect it to be magical, like riding on a pillow of rainbows or some shit.

WRONG.

It's like riding on a – wait, you know what? I think this deserves a list:

Ten Things That Are Less Painful Than Riding a Unicorn

1. Root canal. And not just your average agonizing, cringey, *want-to-die* root canal, I'm talking the kind of root canal where the sadistic oral surgeon laughs (maybe even cackles) and says, "I hope you have someone to drive you home after we're done." Yeah, that kind.

2. That ride at Universal. You know the one I'm talking about. Remember we took Gigi there? There are only two things I remember from that whole day:

Yay! A SUBLIST! Two Things I Remember from Universal Studios Orlando

1. No one should EVER bring a one-year-old to Universal. Like, it's common sense, but more people than you'd expect do it, including us, and so you're plodding around with a wailing, noxious baby in hundred-degree swamp heat, a child who will never, ever remember even a single second of this, and you're looking around at all the other parents who brought one-year-olds, and you all nod at each other in the common understanding that yes, we're all fucking masochists. Never again. (Until next year.)

2. The Minions ride. Oh my God, who designed this thing, the Marquis deSade? They strap you in and start shaking the whole damn place, compressing and pulling apart your poor spine until tears (not of joy) are pouring down your face and you're begging them to stop. And all those years growing up where you wished the rides would last forever go out the window, and all you can think is, "Either kill me or stop this torture machine NOW. Either one's good. Really. Death is preferable to this."

Anyway, back to the main list of *Ten Things That Are Less Painful Than Riding a Unicorn*:

3. A paper cut.

4. Pouring hydrogen peroxide on your paper cut so it doesn't get infected.

5. Having the hydrogen peroxide thing not work, and your finger gets so infected they have to amputate it. Without anesthesia.

6. Leaving the hospital and slamming the car door on your new finger stump.

7. Getting a second infection in that finger (jeez, that finger's bad luck!) so they just pull the whole damn thing off with pliers. (Again, no anesthesia.)

8, 9, and 10. More horrible finger carnage, eventually resulting in death.

Okay, so I feel like you're getting the picture. Riding a unicorn is not my favorite thing.

"So Pete, you enjoying this as much as I am?"

"I think my ass just fell off. In my pants."

"Hey, I've got an idea. To distract us. There's a definite, obvious medieval vibe going on – and the appropriate stench – so we should give ourselves medieval names."

"Why am I not surprised?"

"Because you're smart. Okay, I'm The Earl of Awesomeness. Earl Awesome for short."

"I was going to say Duke of Dork, but sure. I'll be, um, Sir Pete-a-lot."

"No. Sounds too much like Peed-a-lot. Like you pee a lot. How about just Sir Peter?"

"Whatever floats your moat." He grins. "Like what I did there? Floats your *moat*? Crap, you're rubbing off on me. I'm telling groaners. This horn horse must be scrambling my brain."

"It's a unicorn, but excellent, yes, an excellent groaner, my fine compatriot. I mean Sir Peter. If I had a sword I'd knight you."

"If I had a sword I'd beat you over the head with the flat part for getting me into more of your stupid shit."

"Hey! I didn't even want to come in here. She's YOUR great aunt!"

He turns a little and bows before Earl Awesome. "Touché." A little silence, then, "Chip, you think she's okay? Barb?"

"I have a two-part answer to that."

"Christ. Forget I asked."

"No. Listen. I think on the surface, she's scared shitless. But under that? I think she finally got to be the damsel in distress she always wanted. Like in one of her books."

"Huh. I think you're right."

"You think I'm right… and…"

He rolls his eyes. Well, he's in front of me, so I'm just imagining that he's rolling his eyes. "I think you're right, Earl Awesome."

"That's better."

A half hour later. Here's the scene:

We ride into that big square in front of the unfinished Notre Dame cathedral. And it reminds me instantly of what it looked like on TV after it burned last year in 2019. I remember the reporters talking about how it had survived so many potential disasters from its original construction in around twelve hundred, over eight hundred years ago. I spy some dudes up there building the rafters, and feel bad for them, knowing that a single spark is going to undo all their decades of work in a couple of hours. Bummer. But hey, who knows, maybe in this dimension, the cathedral lasts forever. That's what's good about infinite dimensions: literally anything's possible. So I wave and give the thumbs up to the one guy looking down at me. And he's… I can't quite make it out… wait… he just mooned me!

Anyway, there's a crowd ringing the square, some on unicorn-back, one as filthy as the next, except for the upper class folk, one more flamboyantly dressed and powdered and perfumed than the next.

And there's a wedding going on, right in front of the giant doors.

"Aww, look. If Barb's here, at least she gets to see a wedding. So romantic."

"No, dude. Look!"

Oh my God.

Barb is in a white dress with a veil and a Princess-Diana-length train, flanked by guards in frilly outfits (don't let the look fool you, these guys are brandishing some pretty bad-ass swords). It's weird, though (weird, hah!), I can't tell if she's weeping out of fear or… something else. She's staring into the eyes of some good-looking prince type, like six-foot-seven with long flowing black hair and a rugged beard. Shit, this guy's straight out of one of her romance novels. She looks numb, or in a trance. Poor Barb.

Pete fumbles with his phone, madly translating, and shouts, "*Arrêtez!*"

The crowd turns and the priest stops mid-sentence and glares. The guards get into their *ready-to-slay-the-strange-looking-intruders* stance, and skootch a little closer to Barb.

We dismount – or Pete dismounts, and I fall off the unicorn with about as much grace as you'd expect, barely missing a pile of shit, and the locals have to help me up, and my very first step is into said pile of shit – anyway, Pete marches right up the altar, as the crowd parts for him, and Barb finally looks up and snaps back to reality.

"Pete! Oh Pete! You're here!"

"I'm here to save you, Barb!"

I cough.

"We're here to save you, Barb!"

She looks confused, man they must've drugged her or something, and the dude standing behind the dais, in a red and blue cape, advances on us, pissed.

"What Englishman dares interrupt ze administration of zis most holy and prophesied union?"

Pete exhales, he was getting all ready to fight these frilly clowns to the death *and* translate French on his phone at the same time. Now he'll just have to fight these frilly clowns to the death. "I am Sir Peter. This is my fellow, ah, knight…" he rolls his eyes for real this time, so I can see them, "…Earl Awesome. We hail from the kingdom of New York."

"New York?"

"Trust me. Now – hand over that woman. She belongs to me!"

The crowds *oohs* and *aahs*, apparently a few of them understand English too, and they're murmuring in French to their buddies. Just like a crowd in Manhattan, always up for a scene, the more drama the better. Some hunky stranger in even stranger garb from a strange land called "New York" has just ridden into town looking to rescue his maiden. And somebody's probably gonna die. Cool. Grab the popcorn.

Snapping his fingers, the cape dude summons more guards and pokes Pete in the chest. "Zy kingdom means nossing here. If it be true zou arrives to fight for her, zou shall die."

"Then I shall die."

More *oohs* from the crowd. This Sir Pete guy means business. Cape dude sizes him up. He points back to Barb, shaking his finger, angry. "Zou hass claim to zis woman? She is zy wife?"

This gets a big sigh from everyone. *Awww, romance,* yeah, this is the shit. This Sir Pete guy must really be in love with Barb.

"She's not my wife. She's my great aunt."

Now the crowd collectively groans. "Ewwww."

Pete whirls around. "Hey! It's not like that. We ran into her at the hotel, it was a total coincidence, and she just happens to be-"

I tap Pete's shoulder. "I can't believe I'm saying this, but I don't think they need the ten-minute Chip version."

"Right." He turns back to the dude. "Hand her over. Now."

A sniff. "Do not zou knowest whom I am?"

"No, I don't knowest. It doesn't matter. Hand her over."

"I am ze Royal Provost, governing Paris for ze King. As such, I hast zee aussority to administrate zee prophesy."

"Prophecy?"

"Ahem." The Provost dude reaches back and one of his lackey boys hands up a giant scroll, and Julie, I think this guy plans on reading the whole thing. It's like a jumbo roll of paper towels you'd get at Costco. I'm like "tear off a single sheet, read the Cliff Notes version, and let's be done with it." Oh shit. Yup. He's reading the whole thing.

The Great Prophecy and Decree of The Most Noble and Holy Saint… I Didn't Quite Catch the Name
(As recited by the stuffy, droning Royal Provost, interpreted and embellished by the Earl of Awesomeness)

The Royal Provost starts off with lots of *Forthwiths* and *Heretofores* and *Thines* and *Hasts*. In the interests of time (we have a great aunt, two kids, and a multiverse to save!), I've taken all that shit out. Here goes:

Once upon a time, in ancient France, the old wife of a farmer was gored by a rabid unicorn while slopping her pigs. As she spurted blood and slowly gave up her life, she saw visions (not visions of pigs hovering over her, sniffing and oinking, although that was happening too), no, visions of the distant past and the far flung future, and she dictated them to her daughter. And she sayeth: "With mine own eyes I see a black monolith, square in each dimension but tall in height, and it emits a harsh sound, and with its otherworldly voice it shouteth, 'Open the pod bay doors, Hal.' And the colors, oh the colors-"

I interrupt the Provost. "Woah. Hold on. Saint Whatsherface looked into the future and saw *2001: A Space Odyssey*? Dude. That's a movie."

"A movie?"

"Like a made-up story. Fiction. It didn't happen."

"Silence, blasphemer!"

"Whatever."

So he continues, and the very next vision out of Saint Whatsherface's mouth is this: "And lo and trembling, I watch as the sky turns and turns, into a terrible vortex, and the sharks of the sea are swept up into it and-"

"No. Stop. Dude. That's *Sharknado*."

"Stop interrupting me."

"It's a movie, Provost. How the hell are we supposed to believe anything she says? It's *fiction*, dude. Did she see *Snakes On A Plane* too?"

He whips around from the scroll. "Amazing! Hast zou studied zis prophecy? For zere is such a verse! Look hizzer, Chapter 312, Verse 9:" he rapidly unwinds more of the scroll, "'And ze flying machine is filled with serpents, but zine hero holds forss and tears a hole in zee-"

"Yeah, yeah. A hole in the side of the plane and all the snakes get sucked out. Great. Your saint prophecy lady is like Nostradamus, but with movies. Congratulations. Now can we get Barb back?"

"SILENCE! GUARDS!"

So Provost dude has them tie a gag around my mouth, and Pete's like "wow, I can't believe I've never thought of doing that," and then they gag him too, so we just make pissed off faces at each other instead.

"As I was sayess…" and he goes on like this, I swear to God it reads like *Ye Olde French-slash-English Movie Reviews from The Future*, all it's missing is star ratings (or, I don't know, maybe it's negative ratings, like *Sharknado* got five piles of unicorn shit), anyway he finally gets to the relevant part and everyone gets real quiet…

"And on a cloudless day in Spring, I see a woman appear, from ze farzest reaches of the cosmos, adorned wiss a jangly bracelet and strange clozing. She enters ze cathedral and is smitten with ze Prince, and he wiss her. For ze powers of the universe had ordained zat zeese souls be united. Let no man tear ze cloth of their union in twain."

"Mmmmffff."

"What?"

"Mmmmmfffff!"

He motions for them to take off our gags. "I could have you hanged for repeatedly interrupting me. What?"

"I said bullshit."

"Excuse me?"

"Your prophecy. It's bullshit. It doesn't even mention us."

"Ahem. I was getting to zat part. '…and zere will be an ass in ze form of a man…'" and the crowd howls in laughter.

"Hey!"

"…a jester zat will bring mirth and good cheer to all ze people."

"Oh, okay, that's a little better. I'll take it. So what happens to the jester?"

"He dies."

"Yikes."

"Yes. Yikes."

"What about Pete?"

"Zere is only ze mention of a great battle over her, for ze fate of ze universe hangs in ze balance."

"You're damn right the fate of the universe hangs in the balance. We need her for the MERDE."

"MERDE? You know zat is French for 'shit,' right?"

"It's the MULTIVERSE ENTROPY RESTABILIZING DNA ENERGIZER."

He looks at me blankly.

"Whatever. Let's just get to it so we can be on our way and save the multiverse."

"What iss a multiverse?"

"How much time do you have?"

He waves me off, and the scroll falls into the hands of the

lackey – I guess that means he's done – and the Provost claps his hands and shouts to the crowd. "To fulfill ze prophecy, Sir Pete shall battle Prince Jean for ze maiden's heart in romantic love!"

Pete shakes his head. "She's my great aunt." (The crowd "Ewwww"s again, this time it's pretty funny.)

"Right. For ze maiden's *claim*."

Barb runs from the altar, as multiple guards hold her back. "Oh dear, no, Pete. No! Don't do this!"

But the Prince has already shed his armor, standing before Pete…

Naked?

"Okay, this just got extra weird."

The Provost is keen by now that we have no idea what the fuck is going on, so he explains. "Civilized men do not bludgeon each ozer wis swords and weapons. Zey *GRAPPLE!*"

The crowd goes wild at the word, and backs up, revealing a white ring on the ground, I'm guessing the size of a wrestling ring in ancient Greece? Shit, who knows. I should finally stop being surprised by the differences in these dimensions, or temporal anomalies, or whatever they are, I mean obviously some random professional grappler guy was going home to Greece a thousand years ago but got lost on the way, and settled in ancient France, starting that country's professional grappling obsession. We're talking about infinite possibilities, right?

So this guy reaches out his hand and does the little *Matrix* move, you know, the one where he invites Pete to come and get him with a wave of his fingers. Julie, he's built like the steel cables holding up the Verrazzano Bridge, I'm not kidding. His muscles have little muscles, like that pizza from Vito's out in Williamsburg, where you can choose pizza as a topping for your pizza, and your pizza comes out with little baby pizza slices on top. His muscles are like that. I swear to God, Julie, and I'm sorry to say this but it's true, if this was happening to me, and I had to strip down to my naked out-of-shape butt in front of a bunch of medieval Parisians and fight this incredible hulk of a man, I'd just walk away, saying, "Fuck it. You win. It's not even worth the whole multiverse."

But Pete is obviously not me. (Thank God.) He's obviously thinking about the fate of the multiverse, and his great aunt, and our little bumpkins left behind with Tesla at the lab in 1945 Paris. As he strips down, slowly (eliciting quite the breathless reaction from the ladies, I might add), he grumbles, "Rules."

The Provost shouts, a confident grin on his face, raising three fingers. "Sree times out of ze ring and you lose. And no blood."

"What about pinning him on his back?"

"Who are we, ze Greeks?"

The crowd guffaws at this, like those wimpy Greeks obviously couldn't handle real, Medieval Parisian Wrestling. Whatever. I whisper to Pete (I guess I'm like Mickey the trainer from the *Rocky* movies now), "Shit. I was going to say pull his eyeballs out. But there'd be blood. Okay, dirty-tactic-number-two: go straight for his balls. Kick his balls."

The Provost must hear me, because he shouts, "…and NO kicking of ze balls."

Damn. "Pete, you're going to have to win this one fair and square. Sorry, dude."

He leans toward me and, nearly silent, says, "I'm not winning. There's no way. I'm just going to create enough of a riot here, and in the confusion you grab Barb and get out of here."

Holy fuck. Just like that, Pete is willing to sacrifice himself, and stay trapped in this godforsaken dimension-slash-temporal-anomaly, for everyone else. Gigi and Hannah. Julie and Meg. Tesla. The multiverse. I'm overcome. "Dude. I know you're naked, but…?"

He smiles. "Is it hug time? Yeah, I guess."

So we hug, the most awkward *two-guys-hugging-while-one-is-naked* hug, and I think we mentally agree never to do that again, and I promise to come back for him at some point, but we both know that's bullshit, there's no coming back to wherever we are, but I promise him anyway.

"Tell Hannah I love her. And Meg."

One of those very rare Pete tears makes its way down his cheek, God he's getting all mushy, and suddenly something in my brain snaps. "Wait. No. I'm not leaving this fucking place without you."

"We're talking about the multiverse, dude. The *multiverse*."

"Yeah. And we need *both of you*, you idiot."

Wow. I just called Pete an idiot. And he deserved it for overlooking the central crux of our plan: that we need Barb *and* Pete to co-proximity-something-or-other.

He laughs. "Another first. Now we're both idiots. So how the hell do we get out of this one?"

Our laughs turn to tears, as we both realize how fucked we are right now, and how is it possible that the fate of everything can rest on a naked wrestling match? Here we are again, in an insanely-tough spot, pretty hopeless, boy how the fuck are we going to thread the needle on this one…

…thread the needle… "Pete! I've got it!"

"Shhh. Your whispers are like normal people shouting!"

"Listen, you do your best, try to win – and believe it or not I think you can do it – and I'll be the one creating the distraction."

"Should I ask?"

"Probably not. Trust me."

"Oh fuck."

Pete swings his arms and legs around, loosening them up, getting himself psyched up, beginning – against all his instincts – to trust me and my "plan" in air quotes, and he smiles at Prince Jean. Expecting a sneer back, I'm gobsmacked (that's number five, I'm going for the record) to see him smile too, and a totally endearing smile at that. Like this freight train of a man wouldn't hurt a fly if he had the choice. But he doesn't have a choice, at least according to the prophecy, so his smile turns into a little bit of a sad scowl,

the sad scowl of a man who must crush Pete whether he likes it or not.

They tentatively circle each other, near the outside boundary of the ring, and right out of the gate Pete lunges in quick and slaps him across the face, just to get his attention.

Woah. Now the prince's scowl turns angry, and veins start popping in his head. "Je suis désolé, mon ami. Je ne peux pas te laisser gagner" I have Pete's phone now, and take a quick look. It says, "I am sorry, friend. I cannot let you win."

Man, this is fucked up. We're supposed to think this guy is a monster, right? He's being way too cool. Now I can't call him a shitbag. Damn.

Prince Jean sweeps Pete's legs like the bad guy from *Karate Kid*, and Pete falls on his ass. The crowd roars, and the prince grabs an ankle and a hand and literally swings Pete into the air and out of the circle. Instead of cushioning his fall, the crowd parts quickly and watches as he crashes into the stone floor.

Ouch.

"Numero un!"

Uh oh. It's taking Pete a second to get up. But there it is: the Pete rage switch. This guy just turned it on. Man oh man, Prince Jean, I'm not sure you wanted to do that.

They get back to the center of the ring, the crowd's really getting into it now, chanting "Jean! Jean! Jean!" and throwing flowers and coins into the ring. I can't be certain, but I think some lady even throws in her underwear, and before you start thinking it's some slinky stripper thong, remember we're in medieval times, so this underwear is worse than one of Gigi's dirtiest diapers, like the filthiest rotten scrap of rag in history, like why bother even wearing underwear at that point? Anyway, Jean and Pete both look up and dodge it just in time. Then Jean goes to sweep Pete's legs again to the roars of his fans and…

Pete jumps over them.

The crowd, stunned into silence, gapes as Pete uses the prince's momentum to throw him into some kind of reverse waist lock and hurl him into the air. Jean lands square on his back, the wind knocked out of him, and Pete literally drags him by his ankles to the border of the ring. They struggle there for a few seconds, pushing, pushing, right at the edge, until Pete picks up the toxic undies and waves it near Jean's nose.

Jean backs up instinctively.

Right out of the ring.

Fuck yes.

The Provost grabs the scroll, looking for some rule that invalidates Pete's maneuver, but clearly can't find one, so he just shouts, "Illegal move! Ze intruder kicked him in ze balls!"

Half the crowd cheers and the other half murmurs, they can't agree whether to believe their eyes or the Provost, that cheating asshole. But Prince Jean settles it: he marches right over to the dude and growls, "Je ne gagnerai pas injustement!"

The Provost stutters. "Y-y-yes, my prince. I understand your desire for fairness. But ze prophecy…"

"Juste!"

"As you wish, my prince. Proceed."

Okay, one to one. Not bad. And the prince wants to play fair. Bonus. But when Pete rushes the prince, the prince leans down and grabs his arm and does the most amazing shoulder throw I've seen since Chief Jay Strongbow versus the Iron Sheik back at Madison Square Garden. Pete doesn't even hit the ground, and this time slams into a bunch of fans, knocking about eight of them over.

"Numero deux!"

Okay, two to one. Not great.

Time to execute Chip's genius plan. (I know, that sounds like the ultimate oxymoron, but trust me.)

I skulk around the edges of the crowd, man everyone's got their eyes glued to the action, I could run away if I wanted (don't worry, Julie, I'm not running away this time). I gingerly make my way back to our unicorn and take out the old woman's sewing gear. Ahh. A needle and a shitload of thread. All I need. Wow.

That sewing class in eighth grade might actually do some good. I might have to go back and thank Mrs. Owens (even though she gave me like a sixty-seven, I barely passed ninth grade thanks to that angry old coot).

Anyway, as I make my way slowly, slowly around and through the distracted crowd, Pete is taking a beating, poor guy, and Aunt Barb is looking on, completely distraught. But no one, not even Barb, notices me. Good. I finish up, just as Prince Jean gets Pete into a chokehold. He's trying his best to wriggle out of it, but I can see Pete's lips turning blue.

I jump onto the dais. *"EXCUSE MOI!"*

Everyone stops shouting, and grappling, and making bets, just for a second.

But a second is all I need.

I slap the ass of one of the guard's unicorns, and it takes off like a rocket, and suddenly everyone – and I mean *everyone*, except me and Barb and the two naked wrestlers – feels a little jerk, and in that wee itty bitty moment realize that their clothes are stitched together with everyone else's, and all of them are tied to the saddle of a galloping unicorn, and-

WHOOOSH!

Gone.

Everyone's clothes.

Except me.

(And Barb.)

Julie, I can't even describe how stunned these people are, and how proud I am of this moment in my life. Yes, I've saved the multiverse, more than once, but sewing together a medieval crowd's garments and having them fly off in a cloud of ripped cloth, trailing from the ass of a frightened unicorn? Absolutely priceless.

The prince lets go of his death grip, and laughs, maybe the heartiest laugh I've ever heard, at the sight of the Royal Provost in his frilly underwear trying to cover his naked parts, shouting "Zis wasn't in ze prophecy! Zis wasn't in ze prophecy!" Prince Jean and Pete, in fact, are both laughing, slapping each other on the back, like opponents turned life-long friends. But before they get too chummy, I whistle my best New York City cabbie whistle and get his attention.

"Hey! Dude! Now!"

And without even thinking, naked Pete grabs bewildered Barb (and her Mary Poppins bag) and comes running over, with Prince Jean suddenly realizing the joke's over and his prophecy – and future bride – are getting away.

We all jump on the old woman's unicorn, and I'm sure its back is threatening to break, but it takes off in the direction of the door in a cloud of dust, with Prince Jean in pursuit. I'm in front, bewildered Barb is in the middle, and Pete's taking up the rear (almost literally). Barb's sitting backwards, facing Pete but looking past him, toward the prince, almost wistful.

Pete gives her a big hug. "Aunt Barb. What the hell happened back there? Are you all right?"

"Oh dear, Pete. I- I- I don't know. I wish I could explain."

"Please try."

"I Immm. Okay. Have you ever met anyone, and right away, you knew they were the one?"

"Aunt Barb. He kidnapped you."

"I know. But still."

"You're not in one of your romance novels, Aunt Barb. This is real. Well, sort of real. Chip thinks it's a temporal anomaly."

"I know, Pete, honey. I'm sorry. I know what has to be done. And I'm with you. But still. I've never felt this before. Not the romance part, although that's a thrill. No, something else. Pete, I'm sorry to tell you this, but I feel like I'm supposed to be here."

"Yes! Good. You *are* supposed to be with us, In Paris 1945, to help repair the paradox tear in the multiverse."

"No. I mean supposed to be *here*. Paris 1182."

"I'm sorry, Aunt Barb, but as Tesla would say, 'hogwash.'"

She smiles, weakly. "I hope you're right. Because it sure doesn't feel that way."

"Don't worry, Aunt Barb. You're heart's just breaking. But you'll be fine – you've only known the guy for an hour."

She looks past Pete again, wistful. "So strange. It doesn't feel like an hour."

We finally get to the door – oh, and in case you were wondering, three people riding a unicorn is even less fun that two people riding a unicorn – and we dismount – okay, they dismount and I fall off again – and Pete tears off a section of Barb's trampled wedding dress train, wrapping it around himself like a toga.

I have to laugh. "Well, will you look at us. All I'm missing is that tuxedo from last time."

"No time to chit chat. Let's go."

Talk about no time. Not only is the prince on our tails, like seconds behind us, but that orange tear – jeez, it's like a foot long now, and a super-bright orange. Yikes.

As we hurry through the door, and watch it close behind us, we can see the remnants of a prince, broken hearted, lunging for us, crying out for his love, for his future, for the prophetic future of his universe, screaming "Je serai ici en attente, mon destin!"

And the door closes.

Barb sniffs back a tear.

"Aunt Barb. What did he say?"

"He said, 'I'll be here waiting, my destiny.'"

I take a few deep breaths. "*Whew.* Sorry about all that, Barb. But at least we're safe and sound back in Paris 1945."

We turn around.

This is *not* safe and sound back in Paris 1945.

From: Chip Collins
To: Julie Taylor
Date: February 29, 2020 8:19pm
Subject: Re: And you thought talking dinosaurs was weird.

Hi Julie,

Just as I was getting the hang of this infinite multiple dimensions thing (it only took me like five years), this paradox starts throwing temporal anomalies at us, and I don't even know what's real anymore. Was medieval Paris real? A separate dimension? Or was it a ghost of one, like the old version of Tesla we met in the park, or teenage Gigi?

And where are we now? *When?* Is this real? Why are we here? We gotta get back!

"Chip. Earth to Chip. Wake up. We have a visitor."

We're standing in the middle of a savannah in the middle of the night, there aren't any buildings or anything, but it has the same topography (no, I'm not suddenly a cartographer, this shit is just so surreal it's sticking in my brain).

Yes. We're in Paris. Again. I just know it. But earlier. *Much* earlier.

There's a dinosaur stumbling past us, it doesn't even notice us, it's laughing to itself.

I call out to him. "Calvin?"

It turns and looks straight at us. It's definitely a deinonychus. It mumbles something incoherent. Then it laughs again, and makes its way over to us, herky jerky. Taking its time, mumbling a word this time: "…calvin?…"

"Yeah. You look just like Calvin. More or less. Are you Calvin?"

Its eyes are going all wonky, and it's giggling. It gurgles, "… you look… just like calvin…"

"Great. Are you just repeating what I say?"

"…are you just repeating what I say?…" Another giggle. Then, "…you… just… say… more…"

"Chip, dude, forget it, this thing is high as a kite."

It keeps murmur-talking. "Say… more… dude…"

Barb reaches into her bag and pulls out a pack of cigarettes. "I think he's trying to communicate with us. Want one, Calvin?"

The dinosaur looks at it quizzically. "Want… say… more… dude… trying to communicate… with dude…"

"Ahh, Okay. Trying to communicate. Let's try this: the verb 'to be:' Infinitive, be. Present tense, am, is, are. Past tense, was, were. Past participle, been. Present participle, being. You getting this?"

It nods. "I am getting this. Say more."

"Okay, first person, I am. Second person, you are. Third person, he or she is, or plural they."

Pete holds his hand up. "Aunt Barb. The high school English lesson's great, but…" He hands the dinosaur his phone, and it scrolls and taps around (it's kind of hilarious, because its claws are totally getting in the way, and it's high, so it's alternating between laughing and getting really frustrated). Finally: "Ahh. That's better. Yes, I'm Calvin. And yes, I am extremely high at the moment. There's a bush over there, at our camp, we're burning it and it's at just the right, you know, the maximum psychotropic chemical balance, you *have* to try it."

"Wait. Did you just learn English in two minutes?"

"Of course." He points up to his noggin. "Extremely densely-packed neurons." Points back at us. "What are you guys, humans?"

"Yeah. Humans. Looking for answers. Like where we are. And why we're here. Are you *the* Calvin?"

He giggles again, that high-as-a-kite giggle, and calls out past the bushes. "Hey Calvin!"

And four identical deinonychi come stumbling into view, pushing each other, cracking up.

"We're all Calvin. Always. Analogous to your use of the word 'dude.' Or 'bro.'"

"Hey! Like Nikola with the pigeons. He calls all of his pigeons Penelope."

Calvin gives me this look, I swear it's almost like pity, like he's pitying the poor human with the itty-bitty brain. "Um, sure, whatever you say. Listen, you have a particular Calvin in mind?"

"Yeah. The one in Paris in the year 1945, Marie Curie's lab assistant."

"Woah. Hold on. Lot to unpack there. Years? Oh, right, measure of time. We don't have that yet." He taps on the phone for a few seconds. "Ah. One complete revolution of this planet around the central star. Let's see, based on your arbitrary year one, we'd be in…" and one of the other Calvins shouts, "Negative sixty-five million! Give or take." And they all start howling with laughter, falling over each other. "Negative sixty-five million!"

The main Calvin shakes his head. "Yeah, no way your Calvin's here. He won't be born for another sixty-five million years. Our species only live max maybe thirty-five of your years. Even shorter usually. You know. Because we're nihilists. Extreme nihilists."

"Extreme what?"

"Nihilists. Life is meaningless. All dinosaur species believe this, it's written into our DNA. So we wait, eagerly, in fact, for something to kill us, or we kill ourselves early through excess or risk. Weird, I know. But there's nothing like watching it all burn."

"Shit, dude. That's dark."

"That's dinosaurs."

I lean in to Pete. "Jeez. Where is he going with this?"

"He's a philosoraptor. I have no idea." Then he looks past me and his eyes go wide. "Uh, dude?"

"Wassup?" I turn around and look up, and yeah, there it is:
A meteor.

No, wait, not *a* meteor.

THE meteor.

We run for the door and haul ass back through, still hearing a bunch of intoxicated dinosaurs laughing their asses off at their own extinction event, one of them screaming, "Bring it on!"

Fucking nihilist dinosaurs.

From: Chip Collins
To: Julie Taylor
Date: February 29, 2020 8:19pm
Subject: Re: And you thought talking dinosaurs was weird.

"Okay, somebody give me some good news."

Barb takes out her lighter, hands shaking. "Well, we can't go any further back in time at least, right?"

As her lighter ignites, we all notice: its little flame is reflecting on us, but nothing else. It's total blackness otherwise.

"I don't know about that. Are we in space?"

I feel around me. "We're not floating, and we can breathe. It's not space. I think it's... nothing."

"The Void?"

The word sends a shudder up my back.

Barb's whimpering now. It's annoying.

Her hands reach out and take ours. "I'm so sorry, boys. I didn't mean to ruin everything. It was all just so exciting. But now..."

"You never want another exciting day like this in your whole entire life?"

She nods, and starts blubbering.

"Trust us, Barb. Me and Pete know how it feels. Boring is better. That's why 'guy's night in' is our favorite thing now. It's boring and beautiful."

Pete takes her in his arms. "We'll figure this out, Aunt Barb. And if we can't, usually some kind of deus ex machina comes along."

She sniffles. "Deus ex what?"

And at that exact moment, on cue, as if Pete called it into existence, a dot of light appears out yonder, some infinite distance away, but also right in front of us. Weird.

"Hey, Pete, you don't think that could be-"

And instantly the light explodes, impossibly bright, in all directions at once, engulfing us, becoming us, and in that teeniest, tiniest, micro-milli-fraction of a moment we see and understand:

We are witnessing the Big Bang.

Everything from nothing.

Deus ex machina. God from the machine.

We couldn't possibly go back in time further now, because there *is* no time before this. This is the birth of time.

Instantly the possibilities begin to happen. And doors, like mirrors, appear and multiply and reflect every instance and it all becomes mirrors, and we are the mirrors, the doors, looking into ourselves. Our minds are expanding, multiplying too. In short: it's quite the trip.

Barb looks at me and stops crying and smiles beatifically. "Well, *this* isn't boring." And she reaches out and embraces us both, and together we wonder if it's all been fixed, if everyone's safe, and we're in heaven.

But in the next instant the light becomes too much, and too hot, and we're destroyed, completely obliterated, dissolving into…

Nothing.

From: Chip Collins
To: Julie Taylor
Date: February 29, 2020 8:19pm
Subject: Re: And you thought talking dinosaurs was weird.

I open my eyes.

"Holy shit. I need an Advil."

My head is pounding like I just got hit with all the force of the Big Bang – which I did – and I squint against the light and see Barb and Pete squinting too, both of them also mumbling about pain medication.

Pete croaks, "Dude. What the actual fuck?"

We're flat on our backs, right there in the middle of the sidewalk in front of 2020 Rue Danton, Paris. (I assume it's 1945, but immediately scold myself – come *on*, Chip, you know what happens when you assume!)

A coin pelts me in the face. Then another. We sit up, realizing we're surrounded by people now, who must think we're some kind of performance art troupe. (Or they're all still drunk and partying for Victory Day and throwing spare change at every hobo they meet, which seems more likely.)

"Show's over, folks." I get up – which is a bad idea – and hurl, and the crowd suddenly agrees with me a hundred percent, show's over, and they flee. I pull Barb and Pete up, and we're all in pretty bad shape. Apparently traveling all the way back – and I mean *all the way back* – is not so good for your stomach, or your head, or anything really.

Barb vomits right down the front of her medieval wedding dress and starts crying again. What a mess. Pete tries to wipe some of it off with his filthy wedding-dress-train-slash-toga. It's no use.

So I pick up the coins (I know, I just saw the beginning of the multiverse and now I'm worried about coins? Where's your *perspective*, Chip?), and step up to the building, looking over the door. It's red. "Regular door now. Good. Okay, let's go."

"I have a question." It's Barb, all mascara-cheeked, mud-caked, and now partially covered in her own breakfast. God, we all need a bath.

"What is it, Barb? If you didn't get the hint from our little escapade there, we're kind of running out of time."

"See, that's just it."

"No riddles, please. My brain can't take it. Just tell us."

"If these temporal anomalies are like warnings, what the hell – oh, excuse me – what in goodness' name was that wedding thing about?"

"What do I look like, Mister Temporal Anomaly Interpreter? It just happened. It means nothing."

She lights up another Pall Mall.

"Jeez, Barb. Go light with the death sticks."

The cigarette glows and surrounds her face with smoke. "Did you know that Pall Mall was the name of a game they used to play in Paris?"

"Let me guess. Back in twelve hundred."

She nods. "Just has me thinking. So strange. I've been smoking this brand since I was in sixth grade."

A gasp from Pete. "Aunt Barb! You rapped me on the ear when you caught me smoking! And I was in *eighth* grade!"

She pats his shoulder. "Oh, Pete. My dear Pete. It's just got me thinking, that's all. Doesn't it make you think? But you fellas are probably right. I should probably be more like you and stop using my brain so much."

"Excuse me?"

"Oh dear, not what I meant! I just meant-"

"Whatever. Let's go. We've got to get upstairs now."

And every single window on the sixth floor of Marie Curie's building explodes out in a fireball.

11. THE END

From: Chip Collins
To: Julie Taylor
Date: February 29, 2020 8:19pm
Subject: The End.

"GIGI!"

"HANNAH!"

Oh my God. Oh my God. Oh my God.

We're running up the stairs to the sixth floor – no time for an
elevator, if it even exists anymore – running, running, running,
hoping somehow they're still alive, but knowing, goddammit
knowing that they're dead. All of them. That explosion didn't
leave a single person alive.

We're all shouting, crying, running, up and up, and there's no
door to the lab, it's gone, lodged in the wall of the hallway across

from us, charred black. Everything's charred black. The whole floor is just charred beams and black furniture.

It's over. The End.

Over Barb's wailing, I hear a faint groan.

"Hlllllppp…"

"Holy shit. Calvin!"

We rush over, pull off this crazy-heavy cabinet, and kneel beside him. His chest is moving. He's alive. And Curie's body is under him. He must've thrown them both behind this thing just in time. Her chest is moving, too. Barely, but moving.

"The kids, Calvin! Nikola! The kids!" I'm shaking him, and he's got a look on his face I can't figure out. "Calvin! Wake up! The kids!"

A small voice comes from what's left of the hallway. "We're here."

I whip around, and burst into tears, and rush to them. "Gigi! Hannah! Nikola!" And me and Pete pick the girls up and hug them until they can hardly breathe. Nikola is wheezing bad, but he manages to whisper, "What… happened?"

"You weren't here? With Marie and Calvin?"

"No. We were down the road, getting new clothing for the girls."

Gigi hugs me even tighter. "And we were worried, Dad. You were gone for an hour."

"That was only an hour?" I cock my head. "Wait. Gigi. You're talking like a ten year old. And you're…"

Pete nods. "They're heavier than I remember, too. And taller."

Tesla hands me a bag. "Here are their old things. I purchased them new clothing, making sure to give them room as they grow. They are aging at an extremely accelerated rate. The paradox is accelerating time even faster than anticipated."

"Woah. Well, we'll have to unravel that rat's nest later. Now let's get Marie and Calvin to a hospital." I hear the sirens outside already. "Calvin. They'll be here any minute. Is Marie…?"

Calvin turns his body off Marie and sits, breathing heavy.

"She's alive, but hit her head very hard. There's some bleeding. Have them take her. Leave me. As for the device… I'm sorry… we tried our best…"

"No! This can't be the end." Though when I look around, all I can see is The End.

Tesla kneels at Marie's side. "Oh, my dear Marie. I am so sorry." And he takes her hand, and notices she's clutching something. A tube. "The radium! It is intact!"

Calvin looks a little surprised. "Ah, my sweet Marie. You… saved it." He looks up at us. "That much radium would have killed everyone in a mile radius if it was caught in the explosion."

Bobo's suddenly next to me, tugging at my pants leg. "Go away, Bobo." I turn to Calvin. "Is there another lab? A friend of Marie's? Anything at all we can do?"

He struggles to his feet, leaning against what's left of the lab table. "I'm afraid not. But Marie needs medical attention immediately. I'll be fine."

Bobo keeps tugging at my leg. "Dammit, Bobo! What?"

"*GONOSLOW.*"

"Dude, we don't have time for rhymes, or a dance party, or whatever you're jabbering about. We nee-"

Suddenly Gigi blurts out, "He's saying we need to go now. Fast. With him."

I stare down at her. Things are different. By the minute. Much different. "Uh, okay. But we need to get Marie to a hospital, like NOW."

"*GONOPO. GONOPO. GONOPO.*" Bobo's behind Calvin now, trying to push him out the doorway.

"Uh, Gigi?"

"I think he's saying there's still a chance to fix this… but we don't have time for the police and the paramedics. The paradox is going to tear the fabric of the multiverse apart in six hours. He has a plan."

"He said all that with GONOPO?"

Gigi shrugs. "Can't explain. Can we just go?"

I bend over, an inch from Bobo's eyes, and send him a telepathic message: *Okay, buddy. You better be right on this. We're putting Marie's life in danger. All our lives in danger.*

And in one of those super-rare moments, instead of a blink-blink, Bobo's eyes open up, the full depth of them, and I get the message back loud and clear:

We're saving her life. We're saving all our lives.

12. OUR INSANELY LARGE POSSE

From: Chip Collins
To: Julie Taylor
Date: February 29, 2020 8:19pm
Subject: Our insanely large posse

Hi Julie,

So somehow our insanely-large posse sneaks down the fire escape in the back. And in case you're not keeping track, I mean of course you are but just in case, there are *nine* of us now:

The Nine People (Or Creatures) In Our Insanely-Large Posse

1. Marie Curie – world-famous physicist and chemist, and the only person to win the Nobel Prize in both – is currently out cold, probably with at least a concussion if not worse, aging rapidly like the rest of us, strapped to a stretcher hanging off the back of her

roadster as we tear out of Paris like a lab on fire (sorry if that analogy was a little too on-the-nose), the goofiest rally team ever in the history of the multiverse. Bobo seems to think she'll be okay, but Bobo still picks lint out of his fur and drools, so do we really know?

2. Calvin the Talking Dinosaur – Super-smart, but kind of a dick – saved Marie *and* the radium, and didn't kill everyone in a mile radius, so I have to give him credit, and I feel bad, he's got this nasty gash along his thigh, which must hurt like hell because he's the one driving. Yes, a talking dinosaur is racing like hell to the ITA driving a vehicle clearly not meant for seven-foot-tall reptiles (are dinosaurs reptiles?) with claws.

3. Nikola Tesla – inventor of alternating current electricity, and by now you know a million other things, including the ITA, also my teacher, guide, and friend – is failing. No other way to say it. Dude needs a furry alien transfusion or something. Hang in there, Nikola. Help's on the way. I hope.

4. Great Aunt Barb – our official *damsel-in-distress-slash-adventure-seeking-romance-novel-heroine*, and supposedly key to this whole mess – is a complete mess herself, medieval wedding dress torn and filthy, and her heart clearly somewhere else at the moment. But thankfully she's taking care of our daughters – who apparently are now teenagers.

5 and 6. Speaking of teenagers, Gigi and Hannah – yes, they're like young teenagers now. I expect both of them to demand iPhones at any moment, so they can Insta-Snap-Tweet-Face-Tube or whatever those crazy youngsters are doing these days. (Simmer down, Old Man Chip). They're holding their own, though, which is good, not freaking out and fainting every five seconds like their dear old Dad would be doing in their situation. Hannah's calm and quiet, just like her dad Pete, and Gigi appears

to be the talky one (are you surprised? She's my kid). Anyway, I'm impressed.

7. Bobo – our enigmatic furry companion, from God-knows-where – is currently, for lack of a more sane option, our leader. *Gulp.* The instant we realized this, that a small furry creature who humps legs and can't even speak in sentences is telling us what to do, each of us figuratively motions to buckle our seatbelts – which, of course, don't exist. There's no safety net. We're like Felipe Petite tightrope walking between the Twin Towers, and boy it's getting windy.

8. Pete Turner – man, I never get tired of saying it: that dude is a *rock*. Keeps his cool, juggling the nine of us, looks in control even in a wedding-train toga partially covered in unicorn shit. When everything's hitting the fan – and believe me, this is about as *hitting-the-fan* as it gets – Pete's the one to look to. Thanks, dude!

9. And then there's me. Chip Collins. Insanely Large Posse member number nine. Normally, I'd be bragging in a list like this about saving the multiverse – twice – but honestly, shit is a little too unhinged at the moment. Other than Pete keeping my feet on the ground (although at the moment I'm actually dangling in midair from a rope ladder located in the middle of a forest just outside Paris in 1945), I don't know which end is up. My kid and her best friend are growing up right before my eyes (and not in that misty, nice, nostalgic Dad way, more in a *holy-fuck-what-the-hell-in-God's-green-multiverse-is-happening* kind of way). My mentor looks like he's dying. And our plan looks pretty thin. Like rice paper thin.

Uh-oh, that feeling is threatening to come over me, that feeling I hate more than any other feeling:
Hopelessness.
Damn, damn, damn. Like the damn multiverse is stacking shit

so high against us, I'm kind of getting the message: give up, Chip. It's not going to work out this time. You might've been able to annoy your way to victory before, but welcome to the big leagues. Where the game is rigged. And not in your favor.

Damn.

Julie, I won't even say I'm sorry, it's too late for that, and you won't read this, but if there's one thing left I need to tell you, it's that you'd be so freaking proud of Gigi. Her and Hannah are growing up – even though it's super freaky – just the way you'd want, smart and confident and sassy and not afraid of the unknown, and they're cute and just precocious enough to be interesting but not annoying. It's like watching two crocuses bloom on a Spring morning (yes, Julie, I did once watch this happen, from the porch on that horror-movie cabin up in Maine). It's like the single accidental good thing that's come out of this disaster so far. Gigi's got that combo hair, half-red-half-brown, it's awesome, although God they both need a haircut they're growing so fast. And she's got your look. You know the look. Like when I'm at peak annoying (I know, when am I *not* at peak annoying?), and you roll your eyes, but inside that eye-roll is an acceptance of me as more than just a necessary evil, so no, not just an eye-roll, it's like an eye-roll hug. Yeah, that's it. She's got your eye-roll hug. It's a beautiful thing.

Shit. Where was I? Oh, right. The list. Yeah, nine of us. Wow, there's enough of us to field a baseball team. Hey, you know what? Just for kicks, to keep me rational in the moments before this whole mess falls apart and I lose my mind and we all die, I've got one more list (actually, is it ever really just one more list?):

Awesome Names for Our Insanely Large Posse's Baseball Team

1. Insanely Large Posse (Okay, too obvious. I agree. Scratch this one.)
2. The Multiverse Musketeers (Whatever, I've been dying

      to use the word "musketeer" for three books now. Life
      achievement unlocked!)
3. Victory Day (Aww. That one's actually kind of sweet.)
4. Awesome Man and The Brutes (Did you really not
    expect me to slip that one in?)
5. The Paris Paradoxers (Okay, I'll stop.)

So anyway, while we're following Bobo – yes, I can't believe I said those words but it's true – I'm carrying Tesla, he's too weak to even walk at this point, and he whispers, "I've been thinking… about what we're embarking on…" he looks unsure of himself.

"You okay, Nikola?"

He does his *meh* look, and continues. "Do you remember when I asked you to read that book by Carl Jung, and we spoke about the *enfolding* multiverse?"

"Yeah, how could I forget? The last book I read before that was *Green Eggs and Ham,* and you make me read one that's like four inches thick and full of five-syllable words. It was torture."

He laughs, then wheezes and coughs. "…I want you to remember…"

That Time Me and Tesla Ate Pizza and Discussed the Enfolding Multiverse

It was one of those times in the hallway, of too many to count, just conning my way past Fred, solo, and hanging out with Tesla in the hallway. He liked New York Pizza, he said the twenty-first-century kind was better, so I'd bring a pie and he'd try to teach me shit. I don't know if I ever learned anything, but I ate a lot of pizza.

Anyway, on this particular occasion, he was trying to get me into Carl Jung, I guess to open up my perspective beyond *Green Eggs and Ham.* I tried to read it, I swear. But come on, most of my reading these days is movie reviews and tweets. Have you ever tried to read Carl Jung? No wonder he was the big dream guy –

every time I started reading his book I fell asleep like ten words in. *Boooooorrrrriiiiiiinnnng.*

"Master Chip. Assuming you've complete the book," (I nod, but we all know what that means) "do you think there is anything beyond infinity?"

"Woah. Nikola. Back up. I thought we were talking about how boss this pizza is from Ray's."

"Yes. I am wandering a bit. This pizza is delicious. Is this the original Ray's?"

"I think they're all the original."

"Interesting. In any case. I'd like to know."

"What?"

"My question. About infinity."

I stuff a third slice into my gullet and talk through about a half a pound of mozzarella. "Oh. I thought it was rhetorical. I have no idea. Sure. Or not. Whatever you think."

"Come now. Wouldn't you really like to know what may lie *beyond* infinity, Master Chip?"

I put my slice down and use my fingers to spread my eyes open wide. "Okay. Sure. And this time I'll listen. I promise. Toothpicks-in-my-eyelids listen."

"Very well. My friend Carl Jung and I…"

"The book guy. The psychology guy from the Dream Team back on Earth Fragment Five."

"…the very same. As Carl and I were walking down Seventh Avenue, just the other day in fact, talking about the many dimensions I've visited, and our wonderful adventures, he stopped me, looked me straight in the eyes – he's a tall fellow, just like myself – and said, 'Nikola, I believe you are only scratching the surface. Infinity, the multiverse, is only the surface.' Naturally, this led to quite the debate, right there in the middle of a New York City thoroughfare, and– *Chip! Wake up!*"

My eyes shoot open. "Oh shit. Sorry. You have any toothpicks?"

He glares a little, but continues. "To think - something *beyond* infinity? *Hogwash!* As I was about to storm off, vowing never to speak to Carl again, I heard him say, 'The enfolding multiverse.'"

"The what multiverse?"

"Precisely! That is exactly how I queried him. So he described our current reality, the manifestation of all matter, all cause and effect, what we see, all the possibilities, as the '*un*folding multiverse.' But within that, within everything, is a deeper and more fundamental order of reality, forces beyond our perception. The '*en*folding multiverse.'"

"Was he smoking anything while he was telling you this?"

"No."

"Snorting from one of those fancy snuff boxes maybe?"

"Chip!"

"Okay, sorry. So, look, I'm following, totally following you, but in case I want to write about this, you know, to someone not as advanced as me, say Pete for instance, could you describe it in simpler terms? Like with a food reference preferably?"

He looks down at the pizza box. "All right. Consider this pizza slice..."

"Actually, I was considering that one. Can you use another one for your example?"

He harrumphs, but passes me the next slice like a bud, and I dive into it, and he moves on. "This pizza slice. It exists. We can perceive it with our eyes, we can even put it under a microscope, and perceive it down to an atomic level. We can measure the energy of the sun needed to grow the wheat to make the flour to make the dough. We can create fire to heat the oven. We can mine metal to build the oven to make the pizza. But there are even deeper forces, forces we cannot see or measure, that give birth to atoms, that create the potential for the sun, and the metal, and the oven, and the heat, and even the memories of the chef..."

"Um. Can you start over so I can write this down?"

"No. Now all of these things, energy and matter and consciousness, and these *enfolded* forces beyond our perception, even beyond what we consider the immovable force of entropy, they all come together, _un_folding into this…" he holds up the slice high, reverently, toward the light, "…beautiful expression of potential, this glorious pizza."

"Damn right it's glorious. You going to eat that one?"

"Chip!"

"Sorry. I didn't have lunch. I know. Every time we get a pizza you eat one slice and I eat seven. You have an old man appetite, what can I say? I'm a growing boy."

"Yes. You are unfolding. Certainly."

"Hey!"

I look down at my dear friend now, weak, in my arms, searching my eyes. "Yes, Nikola. The enfolding multiverse. I remember. You called me fat."

He chuckles. "You are perfect, Master Chip. But that is beside the point." He squints at me. "I think I finally understand."

Man, I know I'm not going to have a clue what the hell he's going to lay on me, my brain will hurt for a week, but I invite him to go on.

"Chip, I am beginning to see the reality beyond our own. Do you see that blue mesh above you?"

I look up. "Um. No. It's just gray. No mesh, no blue. Just the ceiling of the hallway."

"As I age rapidly, I see blue. And a pattern. I suspect that I am peering into the order that underlies our physical reality. I am looking beyond my physical form, my physical reality, into pure potential. Not the _un_folding multiverse, but the _en_folding multiverse. Oh, Chip, there is so much more to see…"

"Nikola, maybe you should calm down. Bobo's getting us help, I think. Hold on, buddy."

"…I have spent my life working in the physical realm. Solving physical problems. I do not think I have seen…" Then a sudden lurch, his hands in my face. "…the machine, Chip, the machine…"

And he goes limp in my arms.

"What, Nikola? What?"

But he's not listening. He's snoring. I couldn't open his eyes right now with a thousand toothpicks. Poor Nikola. He's aging just like Gigi and Hannah. Just like all of us. Pretty soon he'll be like Tesla's Ghost. *Shit.*

I shuffle up to Bobo. "Hey, buddy. I know time stops in here, but I hope we're getting close to wherever you're taking us. Look at Nikola."

Bobo reaches up and pats Tesla's head.

"WEREHERE."

He turns to the door right next to us, and I watch as he dials in the numbers on the lock:

Zero-zero-zero…

And One.

13. THE BOBOVERSE!

From: Chip Collins
To: Julie Taylor
Date: February 29, 2020 8:19pm
Subject: The BOBOVERSE!

Hi Julie,

Three zeros and a one. Funny.

The door opens with the whoosh.

We step out onto what looks like the rings of Saturn, perfectly flat, glowing, reaching out to forever, but no planet in the middle. Just inky blackness. Not even stars.

And a zillion Bobos! Bobos as far as the eye can see – who suddenly pause their dance party and stare at us. The music stops.

Blink blink.

(That's two zillion eyes blinking if you're counting.)

Holy fuck.

It's the BOBOVERSE!

"Watch your knees everybody. The leg humping is about to get seriously out of control."

But the Bobos don't move. They're doing their freeze-dance thing, like a zillion statues, perfectly still. And Original Bobo's perfectly still too, standing just a step or two ahead of us. There isn't a single sound. (except for Tesla's snoring.)

It's weird, it feels like the Bobos are sharing information or something.

"They are."

Huh? Oh, it's Gigi. I look down, but not much, actually, she's getting taller by the minute now. "I didn't say that out loud. How did you know what I was thinki- wait, telepathy? You've got it?"

She nods and smiles. "I can hear them, too. The Bobos."

Holy shit. My kid's a freak like me.

"Dad, um, I can hear the thoughts that you're pushing out."

"Oh, whoops. Sorry. You know what I mean. You're not a freak. It's a good thing. Well, it can be a royal pain in the ass, excuse my French, and freakishly weird, but it's sort of like a superpower, which is cool I guess. Which means you're like my little baby girl superhero. Super Gigi." And I hug her.

"Two points for the save, Dad. That'll work." And she hugs me back.

"Gigi, I can't hear the Bobos. And forget about understanding them. You can?"

"Yeah. Can't explain. It's just coming in and kinda making sense."

And just like that, the music starts up again, and all the Bobos, including our Bobo, start dancing, and approaching us.

Oh God. Here it comes.
The Ultimate Leg Hump!

It's a leg hump for the ages.

A big, giant zillion-strong bundle of Bobo-verse, leg-humping love.
And it's wonderful.
Ecstatic.
Pure bliss.

For about thirty seconds.

But after a minute, we're all like "holy crap my shins are killing me" and I think they realize they could actually kill us with that amount of leg humping, and they back off. Three or four of them grab Marie's stretcher and another bunch take Tesla from my arms, and disappear, I'm guessing to do some Doctor Bobo magical healing stuff on them or something. And the rest of us finally get a good look at this place.

Wow.

Perfectly flat and featureless. Floating in space. Like a gargantuan ring of light, but not surrounding a planet, whatever's in the center is completely devoid of light. Weird. There's a pull, not crazy but there, kind of pulling us towards the center. And the endless surface we're standing on is literally covered in Bobos. Like a Bobo carpet. Which eliminates any of the sterility of the scene and gives it a weird life and fun, so it's not just a stark, blank plane. It sort of reminds me of that Japanese garden we went to for that tea ceremony while you were pregnant. Remember that? You were so stressed out, needed some calm, so we rented that Zipcar and drove out to Long Island (which actually added to the stress, I mean how often do I actually drive anymore, living in Manhattan? I'm like a senior citizen, veering slowly into other people's lanes, leaving my blinker on for eight miles while I hog the passing lane, and getting honked at for two hours). So we got there finally (after getting lost three times), and instantly the world fell away. Same world, same trees and grass and gravel paths, but man oh man that place was pure calm.

Ahhhh. You were so calm and Zen you even forgave me for farting during the tea ceremony.

Anyway, this place has that exact same feeling, that Zen. (Just with some added dance music and partying.)

And I don't know what I thought about Bobo, whether he was the only one in all of existence, one in infinity, but let me tell you – he's not. There's a cajillion of them. And if I even imagined there were others I kind of assumed they'd look identical, but nope, they all have different color fur, like rainbow colors, reds and blues and greens and yellows and browns and every color in between. And they're taller, shorter, fatter, skinnier than Bobo. God, there's so many of them, though, we'd still lose Bobo in a crowd, and Gigi must know what I'm thinking because she reaches up and takes out one of her pink baby ponytail holders and gives Bobo a little Pebbles Flintstone top ponytail. Perfect.

"So Gigi, what are they doing with Marie and Nikola?"

"Hmm. Not a hundred percent sure, but I think some variation on the *hand-chewing-regurgitating* thing you went through."

"Wait. So you still remember all that? The epic Tesla tales I told you as a baby?"

"I'm remembering a lot of stuff."

"Wow. Can you remember when I proposed to Julie?"

She looks up and thinks for a minute. "A little. Something about her kicking you in the crotch."

"Yeah, that's about right. Hey, do you remember that ride at Universal when you were one? The Minions ride?"

"Yes. You were crying."

"They were tears of joy. Hey, do you remember what I told you to remember right before we came to see Old Man?"

Pete steps between us. "Guys. This is sweet, well, bizarre and sweet at the same time, but shouldn't we be working on the MERDE?" (Side note: strangely, now that I know MERDE is French for "shit," I'm liking the name a lot more. It's like the perfect amount of absurd.)

Anyway, as if anticipating Pete's comment, a bunch of Bobos

have silently gathered around Calvin, and now they lead him off, too. I don't know, I guess they have a spare MERDE-building laboratory workshop somewhere?

So it's just me, Pete, the girls, and Barb – who lights up a Pall Mall.

"Woah, Aunt Barb. How many packs of those do you have in that bag?"

"Well, you never know when you'll be stuck in a… in a… what is this place?"

Gigi's petting a purple Bobo, and it's cooing. She kind of looks in its eyes and says, "I think we're at the event horizon of a super-massive black hole. Like at the center of a galaxy. Is that right?" The Bobo nods and lifts his head so she can scratch under his chin. He coos some more.

Aunt Barb looks around. "Well, I don't know what a black hole is, but it doesn't sound like a place we should be able to breathe." She takes a drag of her cigarette and blows out a smoke ring. "See?"

"We're inside some kind of membrane."

Barb looks up. "I don't see a membrane."

"It's like the largest bubble in the multiverse. I think." The purple Bobo nods.

Barb tosses her finished cigarette, but before it can even hit the ground, Bobo slides under and catches it in his mouth. *"PALLMALL."*

I laugh. I mean, at least he likes the rhyming brand. "Okay, Gigi. So, we just chill here until everything's done, right? Maybe another dance party? Hey, where's the DJ?"

"No, Dad. We've got something a bit more urgent to do. They'll fill us in on the way there."

"There? Where's there?"

Suddenly, one of the Bobos, a green one right near me, starts sinking. The Bobos around me try to tug him out, and I join in with Pete, and even with our strength we can't reverse the pull on whatever's got him. Poor guy (or girl, I have no idea) gets sucked right through. *Pop!*

"Okay, *what the hell was that?*" And as I look around for answers, I notice here and there in the crowd Bobos are getting sucked out of view. Pop! Pop! Pop!

Original Bobo points to the ITA doorway. I turn around to look and *cripes,* the orange tear is the length of the whole side, and maybe three inches wide now.

"It's the paradox, Dad. It's bad. It's creating an imbalance. They're being taken."

"Shit. Let me guess."

"Yup. To the same place we're going. To the Other Side."

14. THE OTHER SIDE

From: Chip Collins
To: Julie Taylor
Date: February 29, 2020 8:19pm
Subject: The Other Side

Hi Julie,

The Other Side.

Yeah, I guess that requires an explanation.

Okay, Cliff Notes first: If we don't go to The Other Side, the Bobos won't have enough time or resources to heal Tesla and Marie, build the MERDE, get it all back to our dimension, fix the paradox, and live happily ever after.

So what the hell is the Other Side? And why do we have to go there?

.   .   .

Gigi's getting mind-briefed on the whole thing by the Bobos as we climb aboard a ship. It's like a huge hovercraft, very shallow and broad, gigantic, but maybe only five feet off the ground, and Julie – it's furry. I mean even in movies and shit, have you ever seen a furry spaceship? I don't even want to know if this thing is alive, because if it is we're climbing right into its mouth without even putting up a fight.

Anyway, now we're inside this furry ship (not alive, based on my expert analysis), gliding along towards The Other Side, whatever that is, and I'm sitting next to Gigi, and I nudge her and whisper, "By the way, Mom would love your hair."

She jerks her head around to me. "Huh. That's so weird."

"What?"

"I don't know, like I just had the most intense déja vu. Like when you just said that, about my hair, I remembered a conversation we didn't even have, about Mom. And about how she'd burp me when I was a baby."

"Holy cow. Honey - we *did* just have that conversation. Back in Paris."

"And did I pat your back and you burped?"

"Yeah."

She pats my back again, and I pretend to burp, and she asks, "Gigi's Ghost? Is that where I just was?"

"Something like that I guess. I'd say stuff's getting even weirder, but you already know that. Hey, when are you going to tell us about The Other Side?"

So Gigi the Interpreter starts downloading what she found out from the Bobos:

In the beginning – *oh, shit, wait, I already fucked it up, there is no beginning, whatever, I'll explain a little further on* – anyway, Gigi's having a tough time getting a super-clear story out of these Bobos, but it looks like they've been around forever. And when I say forever, I mean fooooorrreeeeevvvveeeer. Like what they told us about the Big Bang? They asked me how many Big Bangs there were, so of course I said, "one," and they were like "duh," so I said "eleven" just to be a wise-ass, and they shook their heads and rolled their eyes and told Gigi we should imagine a Big Bang happening every second, and that's closer to actual reality, and the true definition of infinity. And beyond even that? You guessed it: these dudes know all about the *enfolding* multiverse, that field of potential and forces more primary than gravity and light and even time, forces that our physical reality can't even perceive or explain.

I know, mind-fuck, right?

I was having trouble keeping up too, so Gigi slowed down and reduced the whole rambling furry alien story and philosophy into…

THE BOOK OF BOBO
As told by Gigi Collins. Embellishments, opinions, and other annoying interruptions provided by Yours Truly.

Chapter 1, Verse 1:
We are nameless.

Okay, so mystery number one solved: these cute little furballs aren't named Bobo (I think we all knew that part already), in fact they aren't named anything at all. The concept of "names" isn't something they need, as they communicate telepathically, and live and act more like a herd or a hive than individuals. Of course, that doesn't stop me from naming every single one that I see, like Shpritzy the Purple Bobo, and Dongdong the Green Bobo, and Waptastic. I mean, you could name these things forever and never run out of names, because, you know, forever. But dammit I'm going to try.

Gigi interrupts my naming. "Dad. I'm on the *first verse*. You going to do this the entire time?"

"No. Sorry. No more naming. Wait. Just one more, this guy looks like a 'Moopy.' Hey Moopy!"

Gigi gives me another eye-roll hug and moves on. That's my girl.

Chapter 1, Verse 2:
If a leg exists, it must be humped.

Okay, I added this one, but come on, it's like central to their history and belief system, I'm sure. They actually never tell Gigi about the leg humping thing. I guess that's a mystery for another millennia. My personal take? Like their universal sign of peace – the middle finger – they use the leg hump thing as a sign of affection, not knowing that dogs in our dimension do the same thing, but for ever-so-slightly different reasons. It's funny how we can't eliminate our subjective memories when we experience something new. Like if we never saw a dog hump a leg, we might do it ourselves. Shit, now I can't stop imagining people running around humping each others legs in public. Okay, next.

Chapter 1, Verse 3:
If you see a cigarette butt, it must be eaten.

Yes, I added this one too. But I asked about their mouths, like 'why?' And Gigi said the gist she got was that it was a vestige, like our appendix, like many Big Bangs ago they stopped using them to speak because of the telepathy thing. In fact, the only Bobo we've heard utter a single sound is our Bobo. Our Bobo rocks. (When he's not being annoying about it, repeating *BEEZNEEZ* or *STOPDROP* a million times.)

Chapter 1, Verse 3:
We dance.

I mean, of course they dance! But can I tell you, this whole time I was thinking Bobo just dances for the heck of it, right? WRONG. Their dance is a celebration of the intertwined dance of Free Will and Destiny. They believe (and who am I, *barely-passing-philosophy-major-from-a-D-3-college,* to argue?), they believe that the multiverse is neither deterministic nor random, but some glorious combination of the two. That Free Will and Destiny "dance" together forever, sometimes leading, sometimes following, but always in balance.

Well, they're *supposed to* be always in balance…

Chapter 1, Verse 4:
BALANCE.

Oh boy. The Bobos are SUPER-BIG into balance. And here's where we get to the Other Side. See, eventually these Bobos found their way to the center of their galaxy, at the center of their universe, to the two dimensional event horizon of a super massive black hole. And can you guess what they found when they peeked through the crystal-clear pane of that event horizon?

Yup. The Other Side. Or more specifically, a mirror-image dimension. See, the black hole at the center of a universe turns out to be a gateway to the infinite other dimensions – a natural version of the INTERDIMENSIONAL TRANSFER APPARATUS. But the dimension directly on the other side of the event horizon is *its exact opposite.* Where one dimension is ruled by peace and light, its opposite is ruled by war and darkness. Where one is ruled by order and truth, its opposite is ruled by chaos and lies. Where one is ruled by chocolate, its opposite is ruled by vanilla. (Okay, I'll stop.)

Anyway, for a dimension to remain stable, there must be a balance between it and its opposite here at the center of the universe. In the Bobos' case, when the two dimensions discovered each other, the Bobos from our side urged for peace and balance, but the Opposites (being not only opposites but complete assholes) demanded disharmony and instability. The Opposites believed that only through complete destruction of physical reality could they master what was behind it all – yes, you guessed it: the enfolding multiverse.

Now, you know Bobos are lovers, not fighters, but they weren't about to let physical reality be destroyed, so the unavoidable happened:

The Edge War.

Right at the razor's edge of the two-dimensional event horizon, imagine light sabers, and body armor, and dilithium torpedoes or whatever the hell they used on *Star Trek*, and giant ships colliding in mid-space.

Okay, now stop imagining that, because none of that shit happened. The battles in the The Edge War were more like open-field spectacles, hand-to-hand combat across the vast stretches of both sides of the Edge, Bobos and Opposites popping through the plane to their opposite side, and back again, for hundreds, wait no, thousands, no millions- whatever, they lasted more time than we humans can imagine, through innumerable Big Bangs. But eventually the Bobos won, achieving the balance required to stabilize physical reality.

BALANCE. Check.

Since then, they've sent out scouts to watch out for and fix imbalances, to innumerable dimensions, through the black hole. The only problem with this method of interdimensional travel?

It's completely random.

And a one-way trip.

I interrupt Gigi. "Aww. Bobo took that for the team? A one-way trip away from home?"

Gigi nods, giving Bobo a little chin scratch. "He knew he'd find his way home eventually. He says we all do."

Wow.

I imagine Bobo, getting flung through a black hole to ABBA

The Cockroach King's dimension, sitting on a mountain for fifty thousand years, which is nothing to them, just chilling, keeping an eye out for imbalance, and then he sees the ITA for the first time, and then finds me and Pete (and gets clocked on the head with a plumber's wrench), and can't communicate, and watches the whole chaos with Tesla unfold.

Wait. He didn't just watch.

How many times has Bobo nudged us in the right direction? Or outright put his life on the line for each of us? Damn, he got his head chopped off for us, exploded himself into a million pieces in the Epic Battle for the Multiverse, and dove head-first into the Blue Juice to save Gina Phillips.

I reach out with my hands, and he takes them in his, and I finally understand. He's been helping us keep balance in the physical reality we see around us. Together.

I laugh. "This whole time. Calling you Bobo. Sorry about that, dude."

He shakes his head, so I look to Gigi. "What'd he say?"

"He says he likes the name. You were the first being to give him an identity. And having an individual identity is fun. He says it's the bee's knees."

I laugh and repeat it to him. "BEEZNEEZ."

And he whispers back, *"BEEZNEEZ."*

"Wait. Bobo. How did you know how to get back to your home? How did you know the combination?"

He nods at Gigi. "He says he tried them all."

"How- how could he have tried them all? There *is* no all. He'd have to try it like every second forever. Forever."

Bobo shrugs. Gigi laughs. "He got lucky."

And I smile, knowing that *luck* is that weirdest of words, like the word *coincidence*, like do things really happen randomly? By luck? Or is there some enfolding thing going on underneath it all, guiding us, or shaping our experiences? Bobo seems to sense my searching, and he leans over and touches his forehead to mine, and I lose myself in his big, black eyes, and now that forever feeling I get sometimes makes more sense. His eyes really do go on forever.

And somewhere in there, I see a reflection of myself.

But…

It's not me.

"Gigi. What aren't you telling me?"

She fidgets. "Um, what?"

"Gigi, my darling and obedient daughter, I'm your father. Tell me or I'll ground you for the rest of your life."

"You mean the next five hours?"

I raise my eyebrows, like I imagine a real father of a smart-ass teenage daughter should do when he's pissed, she knows I'm faking it, but she also knows she has to tell me, it's just a matter of time.

"Okay, Dad. You got your adult diaper on tight?"

Pete laughs.

"You too, Uncle Pete. Got yours on tight too?"

Pete gulps. I gulp. We both gulp again.

"The Bobos knew we were coming. Not because they can see into the future, they can't. But after the paradox created an enormous imbalance, before we got here, *the two* appeared. On The Other Side."

Pete asks, "The two?" but I already know. I don't even have to ask.

"The two. Opposite Chip and Opposite Pete."

From: Chip Collins
To: Julie Taylor
Date: February 29, 2020 8:19pm
Subject: Re: The Other Side

Hi Julie,

Great. Fucking great.

"We've got a multiverse to save – again – but first we have to bring balance back to the Boboverse? Come on, Gigi. Cut me a break! No. I'm not doing it."

"Dad. If we don't help the Bobos, we don't get Tesla and Marie back, we don't get the MERDE, we don't fix the paradox, and we don't save the multiverse. See how it all works? Together? In a line of causality?"

"Ugh. You're just like your mother. Right all the time."

"I know." She high-fives Hannah and they snort-laugh.

Wonderful.

I watch the sea of Bobos turn into gatherings here and there, then one or two, I guess some loners out on hikes, although what the hell are they hiking on all the way out here? Anyway, then there are none, just the endless, glimmering flatness of the event horizon.

And some unmeasurable amount of time later, the ship stops gliding and lands with a clunk. We step down the gangplank onto the surface of the event horizon. Here it's transparent, and we can see movement beneath us: The Other Side. Our company of about a dozen Bobos leads us to The Edge. I reach out and poke the membrane.

And a hole opens up sucks my arm out up to the shoulder.

"Oh shit! Oh shit! I broke the Boboverse! Already! I'm dying! Save me!"

"Dad, Dad. Calm down. It's self-healing." And within moments, the hole pushes my arm back in and it's gone. Good as new. Or old. Good as whatever. *Whew.*

Gigi pulls me away from The Edge a little. "They've got a, uh, something, I don't know, I think they said a machine, that can suck you in and squirt you out through to The Other Side. Like the one the bad guys are using to suck through our Bobos. Or if you prefer, you can get to The Other Side by jumping out and over The Edge here. There's a local gravitational pull from the membrane that'll keep you from falling into the black hole. But don't slip. It'll cut you in half, and then both halves will fall into the black hole. So you've got two choices. Suck and squirt, or leap over The Edge."

"Gee, I don't know, they both sound so appealing." I turn to Pete. "Who's idea was this anyway?"

And a voice, muffled, comes from nowhere.
"Mine."

Wait. No, it's not from nowhere. It's from under us.

I look down, and through the event horizon, I can see a face smushed up against it, like up against glass. And he's waving the middle finger at me.

Yup. It's Opposite Chip.

Somehow, in this crazy multiverse, there's a dimension right on the other side of this pane of glass where an Alternate Chip and Pete – but not just Alternates, pretty much exact opposites – presumably found an opposite Tesla's lost journal, then an opposite ITA, and made their way here. Opposite Pete's right next to Opposite Chip, also waving his middle finger, laughing. "Okay, fuckwads. Ready to rumble?"

I nudge Pete. "Wow. You're Opposite's even more of a dick than mine."

Then my Opposite turns to Opposite Pete and mimics me, sing-songy and whiny. "You're Opposite's even more of a dick than mine."

Pete nudges me back. "You were saying?"

"Right. They're both a hundred percent dicks. Gigi, remind me again why the Bobos can't do this? Why does it have to be me and Pete?"

"It's kinda gobbledygook, but I'm getting from them that true balance is a delicate thing. Before they can help us fix the paradox, we have to fix the balance here. And Opposite Chip and Pete down there are what's throwing off the balance. They have to be met with equal and opposite force. You two. It's the only way."

I sigh, she's right of course, there's no way I'm getting out of this one, no way I can get Pete to cover for me. Time to man up, Chip.

I look at my slightly-out-of-shape gut and wrinkled shirt. "Hey. I don't get any armor or anything? Laser gun?"

"Do you know how to use a laser gun?"

"Of course." I do my best Han Solo stance. "You know, peow-peow-peow!"

The Bobos just shake their heads and hand me a stick.

"A stick? Are you kidding?"

And then the stick twirls in my hands and moves me around like a kung-fu master in the movies. "Woah."

"It's got something like auto-pilot. They thought you'd like that."

Pete grabs his stick and throws it up in the air, and it pulls him up with it, like a hundred yards at least into the void, and on the way down he spins it and it helicopters him down and he sticks an Iron-Man-style landing.

"Show off."

He grins. "Can I keep this?"

"They said if you save the multiverse, you can have two."

I tap the the event horizon with my stick, tapping right on Opposite Chip's face, still smushed against it. Now he's licking it. He shouts through the glass, "Nice stick, Chip. Sticks and stones, break your bones, Chip."

Jeez. What an absolute asshole.

"All right then, I'm opting out of the razor sharp death leap. Let's do this sucky-squirty thing instead and get this over with."

And Julie, maybe Gigi thought they were saying "machine" about the sucky-squirty thing, but she was dead wrong – it's definitely not a machine. This big worm slides down the gang plank toward us on a leash, an undulating opening on both ends, it's like a giant flexi-straw from your nightmares, I'm not kidding. I involuntarily step back a foot and gag. Pete puts his hand over his mouth.

It sucks onto the surface of the event horizon, and gurgles a little, and lets out a burp or something from the open end. I take another step back.

"Dad. It's easy. You just climb in one end and come out the other."

I shudder. "Oh God. Please tell me it has two mouths. Not two anuses. Those are two mouths, right, honey?"

"Please don't make me answer that, Dad."

Fuck. Whatever. It's never easy, is it. "Okay, Pete. Age before beauty."

"You're older than me, you idiot." And he pushes me toward the thing's mouth (or what I'm praying is a mouth).

So I lay down and spread the thing's lips (again, insisting this is a mouth) and shimmy into the flesh tube – Oh God, I'm going to have to stop describing this for a moment, I almost just hurled, bear with me – okay, I'm inside, at least it doesn't smell like worm ass in here, no gloppy mess to deal with…

Whoops. Spoke too soon.

In the gloppiest mess ever in the history of gloppy messes, the thing shoots me out of its *whatever*, up in the air on The Other Side, and as I twirl the stick around on my way down I fling its mucus (at least I hope it's mucus) all over the place, and onto Opposite Chip and Pete.

They're wiping themselves off. "Gross, dude."

I land in my own (okay, but not perfect) Iron-Man stance. "My gift from The Right Side."

Pete comes shplurting out next and yes, sticks his landing like a pro, even covered in glop. If there were gymnastics judges here, they'd be holding up tens. He shakes himself off. "Okay, good guys are here."

Opposite Pete points his own stick at us. "We're the good guys."

"No. We are."

"We are."

"What grade are you in?"

"Fuck you grade."

"Oh yeah? Fuck you grade too."

I bang my stick on the event horizon. "Gentlemen! Gentlemen. I'm sure we all feel like we're here for the right reasons, and that we can handle this in a mature, civilized manner."

"I'm sure we can handle this in a mature, civilized manner, blah, blah, bullshit whatever." Opposite Chip says this, in his whiny copycat voice again, as he swings his stick around, aiming for my lower back. But with just the slightest twitch, my slightest reaction, my stick turns me and goes vertical and blocks the blow.

Opposite Chip and I stand there glaring at each other, in one of those forever moments. I grin.

"It's on, motherfucker."

And I throw my stick to Pete, as he throws his to me, and on the way both sticks turn in midair and strike their targets. We catch the sticks and Opposite Chip and Pete go down. They look unconscious.

"That was easy." I look down through the event horizon and shout to Gigi. "Okay, suck us back up!"

Well, that's what I would've said anyway. If Opposite Chip hadn't kicked me right in the balls.

I fall to my knees, then into a fetal position, groaning. Pete shouts at opposite Chip, "Hey! No kicking in the balls!"

Opposite Chip laughs as he gets up. "What are these, Medieval Parisian Wrestling rules?"

Pete grunts. "Okay, no rules then?"

"The way I see it, there's only one rule: If you kill us, you get your precious 'balance' in this universe, and maybe, just maybe fix that big-ass orange paradox tear in the ITA. If we kill you, we get the exact opposite – imbalance, destruction, and an invitation to the *real* party. The shit under the shit."

I stand and laugh. "The shit under the shit. So well spoken. Dare I say erudite. You must be a scientist. Or a poet. Or both."

"You sure do like talking, Chip." He nods to Opposite Pete. "Let's see you talk with two punctured lungs." And they both hurl themselves toward me, sticks out, about to perforate my favorite breathing apparati, but all Pete has to do is raise his stick a little and it lifts him into the air, and he chops down, ramming both of their sticks to the ground, sending the two Opposites flying over him.

Before I can even check if my lungs can still take in oxygen, though, the Opposites are up and running back at us.

And the music starts.

I swear to God, Julie, these Bobos, and their Opposites, love their music. They've cranked up some serious electronic dance hip-hop fight music for our little show here, and by show I mean hand-to-hand combat that will determine the fate of the Boboverse – and in turn, all of physical reality.

I look down and notice a little notch in my stick, and some instinct tells me to pull. I do, and the stick extends into nunchucks. *Oh yeah.* Time for full *Matrix.*

I take a running leap and the chucks drag me into the air above Opposite Chip. I slam both his ears and he yelps in pain. He jumps up and throws his stick, and I barely have time to move my chin out of the way, but it catches my cheek and sends me crashing down.

Opposite Chip gloats. "Awww, your face hurt, Chip? It's killing me!"

"Oh yeah? Uh, here comes some really clever comeback."

He stands there. Taps his toe. "Well?"

"No, too much pressure. I have a hard time with clever comebacks when you're waiting for it."

He decides to cut our not-so-clever conversation short and runs straight at me again. But I've got both our sticks still, mine and Opposite Chip's, twirling them both, keeping that douche at bay, and I make my way over to the Petes.

Meanwhile, Pete and Opposite Pete are fighting so close and so fast they hardly look like two people. They're doing flips and shit, and Pete would never admit it, but he's clearly enjoying himself. He's finally found a worthy foe.

I scream over the music, "Hey, Pete! Incoming!"

And he stops just for a moment, allowing me to slip in. Now we're standing back-to-back, almost touching, three of these amazing sticks using our weight and balance and momentum to fight like a fucking tornado, man I've never felt anything like this. Julie, if you saw me you'd say, "Okay who stole Chip and carved him into a skin suit and stretched it over a ninja?" It's unreal, we're definitely winning, we're moving as we're fighting, getting closer to The Edge, maybe a little too close, trading blows but keeping our core. I can feel it, balance will be ours. This rocks.

And then my foot disappears.

I look down and watch as my foot, my furry foot, my second favorite foot, escapes the membrane's local gravity and gets pulled into the black hole, in a spurt of blood.

Opposite Chip is laughing, holding my leg outside the membrane, over The Edge, where he just cut off my fucking foot. "You had a furry foot?" He throws off his show to show me his not-furry foot. "This is what a normal foot looks like, you freak."

I can't help it, I'm getting woozy, oh the blood, but my curiosity gets the best of me and I stay conscious. "You never got your foot cut off? And Bobo never puked his flesh on it? To save Tesla?"

"Save Tesla? We never even *met* Tesla. Tesla's dead, dude."

A flash of anger rises in me. "No he's not! Take that back!"

"No he's not! Take that back! You whiny priss. He's *dead*, you schmuck. And you're joining him." And he grabs my head and pushes it hard, out through the membrane and down to The Edge.

I am literally looking at something so sharp I cannot see it, so thin it doesn't even have a third dimension, like looking at a razor blade on its edge. I'm pushing like hell against Opposite Chip's hands, and I can feel the very tip of my nose slicing open, like a paper cut, and suddenly out of the corner of my eye I see a figure hurtling out from the membrane, past our little local gravity, into the void, getting sucked into the black hole, screaming.

I whisper to Opposite Chip, "I can't move my head to see. Please tell me that was your Pete."

He grinds his teeth and spits in my face. "Yes. Dammit. *My* Pete. Now tell *your* Pete to back off." Another little push, a millimeter further, and blood starts leaking from the cut in my nose.

"Pete! Pete! Don't do anything! I don't think I can grow back a head!"

Pete backs up and growls. "Your move, asshole."

Man, this is like the worst stalemate ever. If Opposite Chip kills me, I mean, that would be the worst outcome for obvious reasons, I like having my head attached to my body, but if we back off, he wins, right?

So I'm thinking the hell with it, if I do myself right now, Pete can take out Opposite Chip, restore balance, and get this show back on the road. Everyone's put themselves on the line for me too many times to count. Time for me to even the score. Goodbye, Julie. Goodbye, Gigi.

"No! Dad!"

Damn. It's her. Gigi. She's inches away from me, on the other side. She knows what I'm about to do.

~~Honey, strange and dangerous things happen out here. Get back on the ship. Now.~~

But before the next thought can even exit my head to her, Opposite Chip grins like he's found a way out of this stalemate. In one smooth move, he releases my head, using it as a lever, and leaps through the membrane, over The Edge, and through the membrane on the other side. Gigi tries to run back to the ship, but it's no use.

He's got her.

"No!" I jump up, on my one foot, without thinking, leaping through the membrane, off balance, and instantly start tumbling backwards instead of forward, my head flipping back toward The Edge. Great. Who needs, Opposite Chip, I'll just decapitate myself! Wonderful.

But then- *"I've got you."* It's Pete, zooming past me, grabbing me by the hair, and flinging both of us, planting his stick like a pole vault, hurtling us over The Edge, and back into our side.

We tumble, stickless, and rush to our feet (well Pete rushes to his *feet* and I rush to my *foot*), maybe ten yards from Opposite Chip. He's got Gigi in a choke hold, poor Gigi, her face is turning purple and she's gasping for little sips of air. He's backed against the ship, keeping all the Bobos and us at bay.

"Anyone moves – she dies."

From: Chip Collins
To: Gigi Collins
Date: February 29, 2020 8:19pm
Subject: I love you

Dear Gigi,

It's true, you know, what they say about being a parent, how your
kid's pain hurts you even more.

I'm watching you now, fighting for breath, fighting for your
life, and I stand here helpless.

It hurts like hell.

It reminds me of that time you choked on a dried apricot while
we were in the park last summer. You were strangely quiet, so I
looked into your stroller and you had this look of absolute terror
on your thirteen-month-old face, you couldn't understand why
air wasn't getting down into your lungs. I've never seen fear like
that. I stopped and pulled you out, but realized in that eternity of
a moment: *I didn't know CPR.* I had no idea how to help you. Do I
do the Heimlich maneuver? Do I jam my fingers down your
throat and try to pull it out? Do I turn you upside down? A
million thoughts raced through my mind, and in those infinite
milliseconds, I hurt like I'd never hurt before, at how helpless I
was against a stupid dried apricot.

By the time my rational brain kicked in a couple of more
milliseconds later, the emergency was over, as the miracle that is
the human body had worked its magic, convulsing your stomach
and throat, getting that apricot, and everything you had for the
past twenty-four hours, up and out.

And on to me.

I laughed and laughed, and swung you around, your puke

whirling out onto concerned onlookers, and even you laughed through your tears, forgetting instantly what all the fuss was about, and I've never felt a wash of love like that in my whole life. Boy, I was happy not to have to MacGyver that piece of fruit out of you, but I would have, I would have done anything to keep you alive, and that's when I knew I was a dad for real.

I would do anything for you, Gigi. I would give my life, or more if I could.

I love you.

And here I stand, helpless again, while you choke for air.

"Just tell me what you want, asshole."

Opposite Chip laughs. "Man, that was too easy. So is that what it's like to have a kid? Even though you know you're all going to die you can't bear to see her go first? Being a parent turns you into blob of mush?"

"You have no idea." I sniff back my sobs. "Tell me, asshole. Let's get this over with."

"Isn't it obvious? You and dickhead Pete. Into the black hole. It'll create the perfect imbalance. Then nothing can stop the paradox. Do it. Now." He tightens his hold around Gigi's neck and she looks close to passing out.

Oh well. I guess I'm not helpless after all. There is something I can do for you.

I know it doesn't make any sense, that all of physical reality will wind up as a charred ash and a memory, but I don't care right now, because in this infinite moment, you're the only thing that matters. I know that makes me selfish, but I love you, and there's nothing else I can do. I turn and hop toward the membrane.

Pete doesn't even hesitate and joins me. He whispers, "You can stop hopping at least. Your foot grew back."

And I look down, and wouldn't you know? A new foot. And it's not even furry. I smile at the irony of it all, that all I had to do to fix my furry foot problem was cut it off, and a new, more Chip-

DNA one would grow back, completely normal. And I find this out moments before sending myself into a supermassive black hole. So I start walking, if you can call what I'm doing with one shoe off walking, and we approach the membrane, and I silently tell you I love you again, and Julie too, I loved you so much, and Pete, and Nikola, and Gina, shit everyone.

We get to The Edge. I tentatively reach out to touch the membrane, so it can suck us out into the void, and…

Clunk!

We stop. Whirl around, ready for anything.

You're bent over, sucking in deep breaths.
Opposite Chip is knocked out cold on the ground.
And standing on the gang-plank, halfway down…

Hannah.
With a giant plumber's wrench in her hand.

Sweet little Hannah, who's barely made a peep this entire time, who's gone virtually unnoticed by everyone, including Opposite Chip, just knocked that asshole out with a fucking plumber's wrench. Damn. Who knew fading into the woodwork was her super power?

I turn to Pete. "Now, don't ask me why the Bobos have a plumber's wrench on that ship, but man, the apple doesn't fall far from the tree. Hannah just sent Opposite Dickhead into bye-bye-land."

Pete grins and puffs out his chest, prouder than I think I've ever seen him. "That's my girl."

You run to her, Hannah your lifelong friend, and you both embrace and laugh the relief laugh of getting your life back, and maybe the life of the multiverse, that feeling me and Pete have felt many times.

"Aww, check them out. They're like *Chip and Pete: The Next Generation.*"

"God help them. I wonder if they'll say 'dude' all the time. And I wonder who'll be more annoying."

"Hey, see that hug? *That's* what I'm always after. The victory hug. Just like that."

"Dude. Check the score. We've probably hugged six times since college. That's plenty. That's six times too many actually." But he's smiling when he says it, still with the proud papa look on his face, and he punches me in the shoulder. He walks over to Opposite Chip's limp body and gives it a kick. "Now, back to reality: let's reunite this asshole with the other one." And he goes over and hefts Opposite Chip over his shoulder, and runs towards The Edge.

Right at the end of his little runway he stops short, and lets the momentum carry Opposite Chip through the membrane, and into the super-massive black hole at the center of the Boboverse. We watch as he gets smaller and smaller and disappears into… into…

"Hey, Gigi. Do the Bobos have any idea where these two clowns wind up?"

"No. Like I said, completely random. They'll be alive, but they're going to have a hell of a headache. Like imagine the headache you'd have if you experienced the Big Bang."

"Ouch. Yeah. I've got a general sense of what what might feel like. Poor Opposite Chip."

Pete laughs as he picks up Hannah and twirls her around. "And poor Opposite Pete."

I clap my hands. "Okay. We got the mojo back." I look down and admire my new addition. "And I've got a new foot again, this time sans-fur, so extra bonus. I'll have to thank Opposite Chip for that little accidental favor later. But now our side quest is finished. Good job, Hannah. Let's get back to-"

And there's a rumble.

And an orange bolt of lightning streaks across the void above.

15. CHUGGA-CHUGGA-CHUGGA-PSSSSSSSSST

From: Chip Collins
To: Julie Taylor
Date: February 29, 2020 8:19pm
Subject: Chugga-chugga-chugga-psssssssssst.

Hi Julie,

So we haul ass back to the ship while fucking orange lightning bolts are crashing all around us, and everybody gets buckled in, and Bobo presses the big ON button, and the engines whirr to life and we're all getting in *save-the-multiverse* mode and–

It stalls.

Psssssssssst. Then silence.
"Oh for crying out loud, Bobo. Not now."
He presses the ship's big ON button again. It sounds exactly like a car with a bad starter.

Chugga-chugga-chugga-pssssssssst. Chugga-chugga-chugga-pssssssssst.

"Okay, somebody tell me this is a joke. Like the Bobos have a sick-but-awesome sense of humor."

Bobo's pressing the ON button like he's in a rush to get on an elevator, I didn't know his little alien finger could press that fast, but shit, man, this thing isn't budging. He turns around to Gigi. *"WEFLEE."*

"Do I want to know what he just said?"

Gigi unbuckles and heads for the opening gang plank. "The paradox lightning bolts are messing with the ship's electrical systems or something. We're going to have to make a run for it."

"Run? We took a *ship* here, in case you don't remember."

"What do you want me to tell you, Dad?"

Hannah holds up the plumber's wrench. "Maybe this can fix it?"

Pete pats her on the head. "That'll get you out of a lot of jams, kiddo, but I don't think this one. Let's go." He unbuckles her and they get up to leave.

I hold them all back. "Woah. Woah. Guys. Are you not listening? That ship covered like two million miles. There's no way-"

"WEFLEE." This time Bobos' talking to me. He hands me a pair of goggles, then all of us, big black goggles that instantly remind me of the ones Marie was wearing when she picked us up back a lifetime ago in Paris of 1945.

"Why do I not like where this is headed?"

Then he hands me a stick.

"Great, Bobo. If I was Harry Potter we could start up a game of quidditch. What the hell are we supposed to do with a stick, kung-fu-fight our way the two million miles home?"

He doesn't answer, of course, and I get the sense he's just tired of my constant whining, and he drags me down the gang plank. Adjusting his goggles, he taps a wee little button on the side of his stick, and four handles pop out, two near the top and two near the bottom. He straddles it and raises it, and a little glow fires out of the back end, and there it is: Bobo on a stick. "Well, there's another first."

"*WEFLEE.*"

"Okay, okay." I put on my goggles and fire up my stick. Everyone follows suit, and within a few seconds all twenty or so of us are sitting there, like a coven of witches from another dimension, hovering on our futuristic brooms, waiting for the starting signal of *Witch-Race-Two-Million*. Bobo floats into the pole position, and automatically, the rest of our sticks fall into a V-formation behind it, and then he raises a finger (yes, the middle one) and Julie, it's literally like being shot out of a cannon.

If I didn't feel like any moment I could slip and kill myself, this actually might be cool, like cooler than the coolest motorcycle. But no, I'm holding on for dear life, and nobody told me that this little stick cycle requires a bit of balance, so of course instead of staying perfectly balanced on top I swing around, hanging from this thing underneath, my ass hitting the heads of innumerable Bobos as we rocket past them at breakneck speed. I can imagine them either giving me the finger as I pass, or whispering to their friends, "Did you see that? The Great One Chip touched me with his greatness!" (Okay, yeah, it's probably the first one, but shit, man, we just helped bring their dimension back into balance, although I'm not sure it matters any more, because that paradox is about to make everything moot. And I mean everything.) In any case, I started counting how many Bobo heads I hit while we were still out in the boonies, but now that we're getting closer to town I'm losing track, I literally am slamming my butt cheeks into more Bobo heads than you can count.

Meanwhile, Pete and the girls are hooting and hollering, having the best time of their lives, balanced on top of their sticks, like professional stick cycle racers, and Hannah's got the plumber's wrench slung over her shoulder, I swear to God she looks like something out of a Mad Max movie, and Julie, this whole thing will probably end suddenly and badly for us all, but at least these kids got to do one more cool thing together.

Kids. It's funny. Well, not funny, really fucking weird and sad, but you know what I mean, it's funny, these "kids" are pretty much grown women at this point, and just a few hours ago they were in diapers, pedaling around the apartment on their big-wheels, squealing as they raced each other down the hallway (and invariably knocking into my shins, adding to my ever-growing shin-bruise collection). You'd be happy to know their squeals are just as cute now, just as full of joy, even at a time like this, and the way they look at each other really is priceless, reminding me again how precious friendship is, that the very best moments of our lives are those shared with friends, friends who can laugh off our shortcomings, and take a chance on adventure with us, and who'll be there standing by with a plumber's wrench when the shit really hits the fan.

Naturally, at this exact moment of fond reflection, a bolt of orange lightning strikes my stick and it shatters into a zillion shards in my hands, and I scream, and my momentum keeps me hurtling ass-down over Bobo heads for another hundred yards at least, until the Bobos part, and I fall to the ground and continue to slide until my head bumps into something hard.

"Ouch!"

Calvin looks down. Disdain. "Well. It took you long enough."

"Hey, Tyra. I was a little busy saving the Boboverse, sorry I'm late." I eye him over, and he looks different. He's slouched over now, and his eyes are glazing over, like he's past his best-by date, and I remember his species only lives to thirty-five. Yikes. He looks fifty-five at least. He's clamping down a metal crate, as Pete, the girls, and the rest of the *Witch-Race-Two-Million* team are expertly coming to a gentle stop and removing their goggles. "Nice landing, dude. The Chip 'One-Shoe' Collins thing must've thrown off your balance."

I give him the finger, which of course was a bad idea, because somehow Bobo must've let all the other Bobos know about his universal sign of peace, so now they're all giving each other the finger, and yeah, that's when the music starts and it's dance party time.

Shit, Julie, I'll never figure Bobo out, but I gotta give it to him – to all of them – for looking The End literally in the face, I mean orange bolts of lightning are striking left and right now, and giving it the finger, and celebrating Life and Balance, and Free Will and Destiny, like a page straight out of the *Book of Bobo*. Bravo, dudes. I give them the slow clap.

Calvin hands me pair of gloves. "Less clappy more snappy. Here, clamp down the other crate. We don't have time for these shenanigans."

"Shenanigans. Where does a deinonychus learn a word like shenanigans?"

"Where did you learn to be a paleontologist?"

"At paleontology school."

He sniffs. "That's about the answer I expected."

"What's that supposed to mean?"

"What do you think it's supposed to mean? Well, assuming you can evaluate and form words at my level."

"You know what, Tyra? Fuck you, mister smart-face dinosaur pants."

Calvin chuckles. "Your friend Pete is right. You're an idiot."

Wow. He actually went there. Motherfucker. I don't know Julie, maybe all the frustration and adrenaline – oh, and the fact that it's all going to shit as we speak – maybe it's all getting to me, and I just snap and lunge at Calvin, while Pete and the girls try to hold me back. "Pete's the only one who gets to call me an idiot!" I can't throw a punch, they've got me by the arms, so yeah, I kick him in crotch.

Calvin looks down his snout at me and grins. "Another fun fact, doctor Chip the paleontologist: deinonychi internalize our testicles, like any *smart* species would. You'd be better off kicking me in the shin. Nice try though. Idiot."

Pete calmly lets go of me and grabs Calvin's hand, bending it back at the wrist sharply, sending him to the ground, wincing in pain. "If you ever call Chip an idiot again, I'll sick my daughter on you."

He glances over at Hannah, who's thumping the plumber's wrench into her palm. Like a gangster.

Calvin shakes himself loose from Pete. "Fine. Listen. We're all stressed to hell. And like I said, we don't have time for this. We're not getting any younger. Let's get moving."

So we get back to work, sort of glaring at each other, preparing these crates for delivery to our home dimension, and while I'm leaning down at the second one, I see out of the corner of my eye: Tesla!

And Marie!

Alive!

I mean, alive and that's great, but not the *holy-shit-look-what-miracles-the-Bobos-work* effect I was expecting. They look exactly like they did before. Which was old. Really old.

"Dad. They did what they could. The paradox is messing with everything. And they're aging rapidly, like all of us. It's a miracle they're still alive."

I look down at my hands, at the wrinkles and the age spots. I peer into Tesla's eyes. He's still in there, but barely. "Master Chip. I had the strangest dream."

"In kind of a rush, Nikola."

"In the dream I went back in time and walked to a park bench, and warned you of this catastrophe."

Woah. Tesla's Ghost. Freaky.

"Um, that's cool, Nikola. But listen," I turn to the team, "everybody, it's time to leave. Let's get this show on the ro-"

And Calvin clutches his chest and keels over.

"What the fuck?"

We rush over, the Bobos too, and Pete starts doing chest compressions. "I think he's having a heart attack. Gigi, do the Bobos have defibs?"

"Yes. Something like that. They're on their way."

But Calvin's fading fast, aging before our eyes, waaay past his expiration date, shriveling up. Marie rushes (as fast as she can, she's literally ancient now too) and puts her hand on his cheek. "Rest, my little one." Calvin lifts his head, as close to her ear as he can, and laughs a little, and whispers, with his last breath, "I loved you. Don't take it personally."

16. STOP DICKING AROUND. LET'S GO

From: Chip Collins
To: Julie Taylor
Date: February 29, 2020 8:19pm
Subject: Stop dicking around. Let's go.

Hi Julie,

Marie's a mess now, blubbering over Calvin's dead body, but
man, we gotta go. That paradox thing has reached around the top
of the door, at least ten feet wide. Only one side of the doorway
left holding on. Yikes.

The Bobos are literally pushing us toward the ITA door.
They've put the MERDE contraption parts on a sled, hovering an
inch or two off the ground, and left space for Marie and Tesla to
sit. So the two climb on board, and we push the whole thing
through the doorway. I turn to say a quick goodbye to the friendly
creatures who just gave us – and the multiverse – another chance,
and I notice: "Bobo?"

He's just standing there.

"Bobo. Come on. Stop dicking around. Let's go."

Blink. Blink.

"No. Come on. We need you."

Blink. Blink.

And I can't help it, I run back over to him and pick him up. "Let's go, champ."

But the other Bobos are holding him back, pulling his legs. So we play tug-o-war with him, real mature-like, and I'm screaming at them, and poor Bobo's probably getting stretched another foot, but I don't care, we need him for this last leg. "Please, Bobo! Please!" I let go, they're just too adamant, and kneel down in front of him. "Dude. What the hell are we going to do without you?"

And he looks up, and points behind me. And I feel a hand on my shoulder.

Gigi. My little daughter, a fully grown woman.

"He's finally home, Dad. It's time for us to go home too."

"Well, shit. This is terrible. Who's going to blink at me now?"

And instead of blinking, he opens his eyes wide, and I understand without words or a mental message, that even though we'll never see each other again, we'll be together. He is literally part of me, part of my DNA, and part of my daughter, and will be part of our lives forever. We are all, in fact, one. I know, that's a pretty deep thought for me, but there it is.

I give him a hug, God I'm tearing up again, like a disgraced televangelist, and Bobo runs around quick and gives Pete and everyone else a quick leg hump, and he looks up at Barb and whispers, "*PALLMALL*," and she digs into her bottomless bag for another pack of ciggies and gives it to him with a kiss on the head. Then Bobo raises his hands in his sign of eternal peace, his curious, weird middle finger, and says one more time for good measure, "*BEEZNEEZ*."

• • •

I'm about to start crying – God, Julie, when am I *not* crying? – until an orange lightning bolt hits the ITA door.

"Fuck. Excuse my French."

So we hustle into the hallway and start pushing the hover-sled like crazed Iditarod drivers (or are they called mushers? Either way, we're crazed) and right behind us, before the Bobos' door even closes, another lightning bolt hits their doorway, completing the tear all the way around. With nothing holding it in place, the ITA door falls into the hallway.

THUD.

Where it was supposed to be is just orange, just the paradox.

No door. No doorway. We can't see the Boboverse beyond. Just the paradox. And then all the other doors near it start turning orange, and collapsing.

"MUSH! MUSH! MUSH!"

So we run like hell, pushing the hover-sled as ITA doors collapse behind us. I can actually feel the heat of the paradox on my bare foot, like flames licking at my heel. I look back, and wish I didn't – there are actual orange flames licking at my heel. I shout over the din, "We're not going to make it!"

And the floor gives out and we're falling.

17. IS IT WORKING?

From: Chip Collins
To: Julie Taylor
Date: February 29, 2020 8:19pm
Subject: Is it working?

Hi Julie,

For a moment I'm proud of my little prediction about not making it, although it was an easy prediction, easy odds, I mean look at us, eight rapidly-aging Masters of Interdimensional Travel, practically hobbling down the hallway on canes, complaining about our bursitis and our next colonoscopy appointment and how Mildred cheats at bingo. It's this feeble gang of misfits versus the PARADOX, a force of nature so powerful it rips ITA doors right off their hinges and can collapse every timeline in the multiverse. Like it's doing right now. We're screwed.

Suddenly our fall turns into a slide, and then a gentle curve, and I open my eyes, and realize we're in a chute, and that can only mean one thing:

Glitter Girl!

Remember back with the Blue Juice thing, those creatures who could manipulate perception to alter the framework of the ITA? And she could mirror back to you what you wanted to see? And make chutes and shortcuts and back doors in here? Yeah – *it's her!* We dogpile to a stop at the bottom of the chute (under normal circumstances it would be hilarious) and Glitter Girl looks down at us, all mirrors everywhere, and if she had a mouth, she'd laugh. But she knows we're in a rush – no, not *a* rush, THE rush – and hurries and helps us get the sled back together, and points us to the left, like a school crossing guard. Me and Pete heft Tesla and Marie back on board, and before we push off, I run up to her and kiss her cheek. "Thanks. You rock." And she pats my head and pushes me away.

And as we get up momentum and once again zoom down the hallway, I sneak a peek back at her – as she's engulfed in orange, angry flames.

Oh dear lord.

"The door! The door! Here it is!" Hannah's waving the INController at dimension number 234,698,594,394,683. Thank God. Gigi, hands shaking, enters zero-zero-zero-zero on the lock and throws the door open. We rush in and close it just before the paradox flames reach us.

Not that it's much better in Tesla's 1947 hotel room. The ITA door is closed, yes, but the paradox tear here is more than three quarters around the doorway and growing. "Hurry. Let's put the MERDE together!"

Without Calvin to supervise, we look like the bunch of apes standing around the obelisk from *2001: A Space Odyssey*, until Marie finally shouts, "Unpack ze third crate. Assemble ze coupler. Engage ze battery. Pete and Barb, please enter containers one and two. Go!" She's giving this the last of her energy, bless her ancient and failing heart, and she actually gets up from her sitting place on the hover-sled and helps us. Pete and Barb cross themselves simultaneously, and smile at each other, like that final goodbye smile, and tears are making their way down Barb's cheek, and Pete whispers, "I'll be right here. Next to you. Look, Marie even put a tube down here, so we can hold hands." And they kneel down, then lay, and reach through the tube and clutch each other's fingers for dear life.

"No, no. Not zere. Here!" Marie's barking orders like a drill sergeant, and slowly but surely, while the paradox grows just a few feet away, we reconstruct this insane Rube-Goldberg device, wires and tubes and a box with a double-shielded tube of *just-dangerous-enough-to-kill-everything-within-a-mile* radium, and two coffins. I look through the window of the one nearest me. "You hanging in there, Aunt Barb?"

She's shaking. "Can I have one last Pall Mall?"

Marie scolds her. "Are you crazy? Zis device and its fuel are so volatile, you would have to be insane…" and she looks around at The End of Everything, "…Oh what ze hell. Why not?" And she takes two cigarettes out of Barb's purse, lights them, opens Barb's coffin and hands her one, then clamps it shut and takes a drag of the other one. "Ahh. Pall Mall. My favorite. You know, it was a game played-"

"Yeah, yeah, back in old-timey Paris, got it. We ready, Marie?"

She nods. I look down, I can see Pete, he gives me the thumbs up, but Barb's now hidden in a cloud of cigarette smoke. I assume she's in there and fine, now that she's literally smoking like a chimney. The battery is heating the radium (or doing something, I swear they explained this whole thing to me a dozen times and every single time I was like "why are you wasting your breath? There's not a test at the end, is there? I'm not going for my radiology degree.") And the lights above the little toggle switches all turn green.

Marie drops her cigarette to the floor and puts it out with her toe, reaches over to the switches. "Nikola. In honor of my lost little Calvin… will you help me do the honors?"

He stands, stiff and awkward, and walks over to us. "Yes, Marie. It would be my honor. Three, two, one-"

"Wait. Are we going on one? Or go?"

"Go."

"Are you telling me that's when we'll do it, are are you actually saying 'go?'"

He smiles, still a chuckle left in the old man, and winks at her. "Go."

And they flick all the toggle switches.

Silence.

Tesla and Marie stare at each other. "Marie, I hadn't calculated the sonic vibrations the MERDE would make. It is awfully quiet. I cannot believe I am asking this, but… is it working?"

She raises an eyebrow. "I- I don't know."

And, as if in answer, a voice starts talking, from somewhere in the mess of tubes and wires and radium.

It's Calvin.

"Ahem. If this recording is playing, it means I did not make the party to tell you all in person. Too bad. I would have loved to see the looks on your faces. Not that I hate you, don't take it personally, it's not a personal vendetta, but as a species, you just don't get it, do you? Even Marie, Madame Curie, my dear surrogate mother, I loved you, I truly did. But you couldn't nurture out of me the desire, oh, as much love as you gave me, you couldn't extinguish this white-hot desire that's been smoldering in my heart since the day I was born, for self destruction. It almost worked, I've tried, believe me, but in fact, it's only gotten hotter. I don't love myself for what I am. I've struggled my entire life with it. But I am what I am. So no, the intricate, genius, multiverse-saving device we built will not work, not now or ever. I made some last-minute adjustments to ensure that. And regrettably, I won't be able to join you while you *WATCH IT ALL BURN*."

I start ripping out wires and shit, trying to stop Calvin. "Shut up, you fucking nihilist dinosaur! You fucking killed us! You killed us all!" I'm weeping now, weeping for everyone in the room, my daughter, my friend, my mentor, for you Julie, and for everyone that will never know another day. "You fucking killed us, you piece of shit!" I'm banging on the device, pulling it apart, breaking it to pieces. "No! No! It can't be over!" I turn in a rage to Tesla, wild-eyed.

"Tell me it's not over!"

He's crying now too, I've never seen him cry, maybe he's never cried before, but now it's the last thing he'll ever do. I stop raging, and hold his face in my hands. "Nikola. Tell me it's not over. Please."

He looks into my eyes, tears streaming down both our faces. "Master Chip. I have failed. I have come all this way… only to fail." He sobs and searches my eyes.

And something changes.

I'm watching the man I've admired more than any other, the father I didn't have as I reached manhood, the guy who's saved me more times than I can count, in more ways than I can count, wither in front of me, claiming he's a failure. Nikola Tesla. A failure.

No.

That will *not* be the last thing that happens.

"Nikola, listen. You didn't fail."

He's shaking his head, wheezing now.

"You didn't fail. Look at what you've created. Everywhere! You invented it all. You even invented a portal to the multiverse!" I'm wiping his tears as he looks down and his head relaxes in my hands. "And- and- and you invented *me*."

He looks up, raises an eyebrow.

"Yes! You invented me, Nikola. Look who I am today. I've grown so much. And loved so much. There isn't a day that goes by that I don't thank my lucky stars I found you. I mean, look how much pizza you let me eat. No really, I'm not kidding – I've become who I am, thanks to you."

Now he's wiping my tears. "If it were so, Chip, you would be my greatest achievement. I love you, son." And he leans forward, tousles my hair, and kisses me on my forehead.

Gigi approaches and puts her arms around both of us.

And suddenly her voice is in my head, and Nikola's, the three of us are connected telepathically.

~~Nikola. Dad. We didn't fail. And I don't mean in a metaphorical way. I mean in a literal way. Listen.~~

By now the others have joined our circle, all surrounding and holding Tesla. Marie, distraught now not only from Calvin's death but his betrayal, weeping on Tesla's shoulder, and Pete and Barb out from their coffins, and Hannah, sweet, silent Hannah, all in the last embrace. Gigi has added their minds to our little mental conference call. It's scary as hell, actually, but beautiful at the same time.

~~I don't know exactly how I know this, guys, but I do: the MERDE was never going to work. It wasn't supposed to work. Nikola, you and Marie pursued that solution because it made sense in the physical world, the unfolding multiverse. It made sense that the paradox was a problem to solve.~~

She smiles, a hopeful smile, at the center of The End, and she strokes Tesla's hair and speaks out loud.

"Nikola, the paradox isn't the problem. *The paradox is the solution.*"

He looks at her, confused, man, I've never seen him confused either, it's a weird look for him. Like a second-grade science teacher whose student just showed him the theory of relativity scribbled in her composition notebook. The gears start turning again, I can see them in his eyes, thank God, but he can't quite get the answer. "Gigi, if the paradox is the solution, what is the problem?"

"Barb."

We all turn to Barb.

"Me?" And she faints. Barb go boom.

"The paradox is the solution to an even more primary problem, an *enfolding* problem. Just like the Bobos say, there is a dance, a dance of Free Will and Destiny. We have shaped our own lives, and saved the multiverse, all through our own free will, but there was a deeper destiny that was broken. A deeper balance that was off. And Barb is the key."

A lightbulb goes on in my head. (It's a dim one, but I'm still counting it as a lightbulb.) "Paris?"

"Yes, Dad. Great Aunt Barb was meant to be in Paris in 1182. Her existence in our dimension, on this timeline, was a mistake. Now I don't know how the enfolding multiverse makes a mistake like that, but she was supposed to get married to Prince Jean, a very long time ago, and have children, and their children were supposed to have children, and on and on and on."

"Why?"

"I'm not sure. I can't see the future. It hasn't unfolded yet. But the vibe I get is that it has something to do with me. Being a mother."

"Woah. My two-year-old daughter is talking about having kids already. Ah, they grow up so fast."

She grins and turns back again to Tesla. "So you Nikola, by creating the INTERDIMENSIONAL TRANSFER APPARATUS, and accidentally creating a paradox, and collapsing all timelines and dimensions, have given the deeper part of the multiverse, the enfolding part, a way to get Barb back where she belongs. You didn't fail. You succeeded."

Tesla exhales, and smiles wide. A winning smile.

And then he shuts his eyes.

And slumps in my arms.

I lead him to the nearest chair, his farting chair, and sit with his frail form across my lap.

"Please don't go, Nikola. Please don't go." I'm rocking him back and forth, back and forth. I try to send him a little telepathic thought, but get no response. I look up to Gigi. "Is he gone?"

She nods.

But then she tells me a story, one of Nikola's animal stories, using her mind, in his voice:

"Once there was a squirrel, he pranced from tree limb to tree limb, exploring his little world, gathering nuts, chasing girl squirrels, and making hay for all to see. One day he was surprised to find his mother in a bundle on the ground. 'Mother, are you all right?' he asked. But she wasn't. She had passed away in the night. The little squirrel was heartbroken and lived many days in a sad, lonely state. His friends left him, even the light he carried around in his heart left him. He was nothing, almost.

Then one morning a light shone in his window – the light of a new day, streaming in, surprising him with its brilliance, and he realized that life is an honorable thing, just the everyday living of life, it honors the ones we've left behind, and honors the living too, and time, and the heavens. So he walked out of his little home, for the first time in a while, and stretched, and scampered down the tree to the ground, where once again he stood at the place where his mother lay buried. "I will live on, Mother. And I will remember that you loved me above all things." He listened closely, for he thought he heard her voice, whispering in his ear. She said, 'Then I shall live forever.'"

Gigi reaches down and says aloud, "There's a lot I don't know, Dad. But I know we live forever."

Wow. Julie, it's official: our little daughter has become something beyond our wildest dreams, something even more than a Master of Interdimensional Travel. I don't even know what she's become actually, but I'm literally in awe. We're all sitting or standing around watching her, she's almost glowing. Marie sits in the little chair by the window, and whispers, "…thank you, Gigi… for ze hope…" and age takes her, and she closes her eyes and drifts into forever along with Nikola.

The orange tear reaches the end of the doorway and engulfs it in flame. The door falls into the hallway with a thud. Spidering out from the doorway, the paradox rips the wallpaper, reaching across towards us.

"That's my cue. Barb, come with me." She reaches down, waking Aunt Barb from her daze, and pulls her up standing. "Pete, say goodbye."

Pete, faltering from age, coughs and protests. "No. I should do it. It was supposed to be me and Barb. The two of us. That little electric arc or whatever it was. It won't work without the two of us."

Gigi's hands rest on his shoulders. "Uncle Pete. Sorry to tell you this, but it's not you." She takes Barb's arm and holds up her wrist, the bracelet jangling. "It was the charm. The heart charm. It was telling the paradox it had done its job. The two copies were together again. But they aren't yet, are they?"

Pete goes for his pants pocket to reach for his keys, but he can't, because he doesn't have pockets anymore, just a wedding-dress-train-toga. And his eyes widen in understanding. "I left my keys in my pants. Back in…"

Gigi nods. "Paris, 1182." She puts Barb's hands in Pete's. "Now say your goodbyes."

Pete takes Barb in his arms. She pulls a quarter magically from behind his ear and puts it in his shirt pocket. "Now don't go spending all that on pretty girls." And she reaches up and pulls his earlobe.

And Pete, my best friend and now an old, old man himself, cries like a baby.

Hannah leads him away, next to us on the fainting couch. Gigi leans down and kisses us both on the head. "I'll be back before you know it, Old Men."

And we watch as Gigi takes Barb's hand and walks confidently into the paradox.

Goodbye, Gigi.
Please come home.

18. MENTAL NOTE

Mental Note
From: Gigi Collins
To: Dad
Date: I have no idea

Dear Dad,

I have a lot to tell you, and I'd like to say we'll catch up when I get back, but I'm not sure I get a return trip on this ticket. I think this destiny thing might be one way. But I'll try to package up this little note and get it to you somehow before… whatever.

First, I want to come clean about your wedding ring.

You took a lot of heat from Mom about losing it, and I know you thought you lost it, because that's like you to lose important stuff, but that's not what happened.

I flushed it down the toilet.

I understand if you're pissed, but remember that I wasn't even two years old yet. I had just learned about pulling the lever and making the water go *whoosh*, and your ring looked like it wanted to go for a ride. It won't happen again, I promise.

Second, about the dried apricot thing – it wasn't your fault. I know it's probably normal to carry around guilt like that our whole lives, but really, as my mind grows and expands, and I learn at this incredible pace, I can tell you one thing: shit happens. That's the beauty and the danger of Free Will. It allows us to find our way in the multiverse, but also to make mistakes, little and big, from stubbing our toes to accidentally killing ourselves. And it's no one's fault. So you can let that one go, Dad, actually you can let all of them go, all the guilt for all the stupid stuff you think you've done.

And that's the main point I think I'm trying to get to: that I won't remember all the stupid stuff – although maybe I will, just for a laugh – what I'll really remember are all the wonderful little moments you and Mom shared with me. Like that day at the dinosaur park in Florida. You weren't kidding when you said that was one of my favorite things, Dad. I dreamed about that park, and riding dinosaurs, for weeks after that. I dreamed about owning a dinosaur zoo and petting them and sharing them with Hannah. Of course, now I know better, that dinosaurs are train wrecks, and helpless against their own self-destructive instincts, and I will definitely be steering clear of any I may meet in the future. If there is a future for me.

I'll also remember that time you took Hannah and I to the Hamilton kiddie pool down on the Lower East Side last summer. It was the first time I had seen so much water, it was like the ocean to me, and you smeared me with sunscreen but you missed a spot right on my foot and I had a red foot for two weeks. But it didn't matter, we were both splashing and giggling and you were acting like a shark, like only a dad could do, in a foot of water, and the sun seemed warm enough to last forever, and everything was color and water and love.

Oh, and how will I ever forget my first birthday party, where you made that cake that I was supposed to taste and smear all over my face, but instead Mrs. Rosen's dog jumped up and snagged it off the high chair, running around the apartment trying to gobble it down before anyone could catch her, leaving a trail of gooey chocolate mixed with dog slime that took you guys a week to clean up. I'll never forget watching you two, taking turns scrubbing the area rug in the living room, whispering, "Happy Birthday!" to each other, knowing you'd never say it the same way again, laughing and falling into each other's arms, and rolling around chuckling like little kids yourselves. Even then, Dad, you and Mom showed me so much about love.

Gosh, Dad, I'll remember it all, there's so much more, and I hope there's more to come. Because I've grown up in a matter of hours, years of my life compressed into minutes, I'm hoping like the bellows on an accordion, it'll stretch out again and fill in all the spaces with music and memories.

But even if it doesn't, Dad, I wanted to say thank you.

Thank you for taking me to see Old Man one more time. Nikola Tesla really was one in a million, and you were willing to take a chance – which turned out to be the ultimate chance – to make it happen.

Thank you for watching out for the multiverse these past few years. I'm not sure you'll ever get the credit you deserve, with all the FBI coverup-slash-misinformation, but really, you did a bang-up job. (Plus, I'm sure you'll try to give yourself credit at every opportunity you get, am I right?) Like with that guy WHO – what an absolute creep. You showed him. And the Blue Juice? We all would've had a pretty nasty blue future if it wasn't for you, Mister President.

And thank you, Dad, for loving me. I know that sounds strange, like love isn't something you thank someone for, but I don't care. Thank you. Because love – and this is one of the things I know for sure – powers everything, whether it's enfolding or unfolding, before time, through time, and after time.

And you've given all of yours to me.

I love you, Dad.

. . .

"Are you all right, Gigi?"

It's Barb. Wiping a tear from the corner of my eye.

"Yes, Barb. I was, um, just packaging something up for somebody."

We're walking, down the same familiar hallway of the INTERDIMENSIONAL TRANSFER APPARATUS, but also not the same. Totally different. Imagine being able to see *inside* the hallway, at the potentials and forces creating it all. That's what we're seeing. Orange, fiery, but strangely not burning us. I don't think it has a consciousness, not like ours anyway, but something senses our presence, our purpose, and is letting us pass.

"Oh dear. Look at you, Gigi. Those clothes are for a teenager. And you're a grown woman now."

I laugh. "Yeah. Pretty tight. Uncomfortable. But not as uncomfortable as that medieval wedding dress looks."

"You'd be surprised. It fits me like a glove." She twirls around, allowing it to billow out and brush against me.

"Well, then let's get you to the chapel." And I turn the next left.

"How do you know where we're going? We don't have an INController."

"Um, I don't know if I can explain. It's sort of like I can see a map in my mind."

"Of the whole thing?"

"No. Just the part in front of me, and where I'm headed. Like if I concentrate on my destination, it pulls and pushes me, like the needle on a compass."

We walk like this for a while, turning left, right, this way and that, taking elevators, peering into doorways along the way, not that they show us anything, they're just orange like everything else.

"What happened to them? The dimensions?"

"They're waiting."

"For what?"

"For you. No pressure, Great Aunt Barb. Just the entire multiverse, unfolding and enfolding, they're all waiting for you." I wink at her.

"Oh dear."

"Don't faint, Barb. Not now."

Another silent few moments. Then, "Gigi, is there- is there… anything inside this? Like *inside* the inside? Does it keep going?"

"Great question, Barb. I have no idea." I look up. "Maybe this thing knows."

Floating a foot or so above three doors we're facing is a figure, formed by the undulating orange flames. It's the top half of what looks sort of human. In a loud voice, it announces, "Welcome to your Destiny."

Then it just floats there for a while, silent.

"I'm not sure, are we supposed to bow or something?"

It looks down and smiles. "Not necessary. Allow me to introduce myself. I am… The Plumber."

I snort. I can't help it. "You're kidding."

Barb chuckles. "The Plumber?"

The figure scowls. "What. You don't like it?"

"Well, it's just that, you're some kind of ethereal god-like being made up of paradoxical, enfolding multiverse orange flames, that's like the last name I would've expected. To be honest, I wasn't even expecting a name. Or maybe a name that couldn't be uttered or something."

"I like names. Names that *can* be uttered. My utterable name is The Plumber."

We both snort now, Barb and I, and I don't know why, we can't help it, it turns into one of those giggle fits, I think we're both trying to imagine this beautiful, godlike creature strapping on a tool belt and bending over the kitchen sink, showing its ass-crack. The poor Plumber is looking flustered and embarrassed.

"Look, you two. It makes perfect sense. I even used a

metaphor *from your own dimension* to manifest! Come on, cut me some slack."

"Sorry. So… can you explain?"

"Imagine you are in a house. The house looks and runs perfectly. Why?"

I start to understand. "Because it's got plumbing?"

"*Exactly.* All the stuff you don't see, plumbing, wiring, air conditioning, insulation. The stuff behind the stuff. The house only works because it's got plumbing. That's why I'm The Plumber."

Barb raises her hand, excited. "Oooh! Oooh! So I have a question… is there stuff inside the stuff? Like is there something inside the plumbing that makes the plumbing work? Is there a reality inside *your* reality which is inside *our* physical reality?"

The Plumber fidgets uncomfortably. "I… I… I am not at liberty to say."

I laugh. "You don't know, do you?"

It glares down at me, miffed. "Look, a few hours ago you were worried about pooping in your diaper…" then glares at Barb, "…and you had your nose in ten different romance novels. Now you want to know about levels of reality within levels of reality?"

"You don't know, do you?"

"Shush. It doesn't matter." A bolt of orange lightning strikes the floor right in front of us with a loud *CRACK!* "Now. Choose a door. They're waiting." It points down. (Oh, The Plumber has three arms now, by the way, one for each door.)

I stare at the doors. "Hold on. You're going to base the fate of the entire multiverse and all time and physical reality on a random choice?"

"Free Will."

"I thought it was our Destiny."

"It's a dance. Come, Gigi. Free Will and Destiny. Together. That much you know already."

I pace back and forth in front of the doors.

"Hmmm. Okay, I'll buy that. But why does free will have to be random? We're not talking about luck. Like the lottery. Why randomly choose a door?"

"Because if you knew the outcome of your choice, it wouldn't be free will now, would it?"

Barb nods and whispers, "Fair point. It's got a point. And it's fair."

"No. That's apples and oranges. Okay, The Plumber, when I have a choice between outcomes, I make it based on inputs, context, knowledge of the risks. Not random, blind choices. This isn't the same."

"Most of the choices you make in life are based on incorrect assumptions, bad data, or totally irrelevant context that has no bearing on the outcome. You are blind. Choose a door."

"No. I'm not done yet. Most of the choices I make in life are binary. Yes or no. Go to Subway and get a sandwich or eat the leftover half sandwich in the fridge. Take a shower or stay in my jammies. Yes or no. There should be two doors, not three."

The Plumber shrugs. "Fine. You're a real pain in the ass, you know that?"

And one of the doors disappears.

Two doors.

A fifty-fifty chance.

One side of the coin, everyone wins. The other side, well – game over.

It's not fair.

Or as you would say, Dad - this is bullshit.

Wait.

You know what you'd say?

You'd say that there's always a way around the rules. You'd tell me to cut the coin down the middle so you get heads *and* tails. You'd tell me to make up an outrageous story on live TV to get your hands on a rhodium asteroid. You'd tell me to sew a bunch of people's clothes together and tie them to a surprised unicorn to get out of medieval Paris and race home. (Okay, that one's kind of a stretch, I admit.)

Two doors.

And two of us.

I turn to Barb, and I don't even have to send her the thought saying, "left," and she grins.

And she runs to the left door, and I run to the right, and we throw them both open.

The Plumber shouts, "No! That's against the rules! You weren't- I mean how in hell- Wait, what the fu-"

But while The Plumber tries to unscramble its own brain and make sense of what we just did, we each stand in front of an open doorway.

Barb is bathed in afternoon light, looking down, tears rolling down her face, at her long-lost love, Prince Jean, exactly where you and Uncle Pete last left him, groveling in the mud as his beloved, his destiny, disappeared through a strange doorway. And now here she is again, magically reappearing before him, and he stands. She is old, an old woman now, but it doesn't matter. Love doesn't care about age or time. He holds up Uncle Pete's keys, delicately unclasping the heart charm engraved with a T, and holds it up to an identical one, brand new, hanging from a chain around his neck. Barb reaches out her hand, jangling her bracelet, letting her own heart join with his, together at last, as they were always meant to be.

She looks over to me, winks, and whispers, "Thank you, Gigi. Oh, listen, there are a couple more packs of Pall Malls in here if you decide to take up smoking." Then she hands me her Mary Poppins bag, and takes Jean's hand, stepping into yesterday, into some dimension somewhere, quickly becoming the young maiden she was when we left on this great adventure.

"Goodbye Barb." I blow her a kiss.

And I look up at The Plumber, and its face has changed, still so mysterious, but now the slightest hint of a wry smile, like Mona Lisa's smile, the smile of someone that knows something that no one else will ever know.

Then I turn back to my own choice, the open doorway in front of me, and realize:

It's home.

It's still 1947 in there. Tesla's time. Tesla's hotel room.

There is still something left to be done.

Bodies lie on the floor, old, tired, or lifeless, and Hannah, with Uncle Pete's head in her lap, weeps.

And next to her…

My father.

You, Dad. The man I admire more than any other. My mentor and friend. The guy who's saved me more times than I can count, in more ways than I can count.

You're about to die.

But I'm coming, Dad. I'm coming home.

19. MAN, GETTING OLD SUCKS

From: Chip Collins
To: Julie Taylor
Date: February 29, 2020 8:19pm
Subject: Man, getting old sucks.

Hi Julie,

My breath is heavy. Everything hurts.

Man, getting old sucks.

I'm an antique now, turning into a ghost myself.

"Hey, Pete. Want to join my shuffleboard team? I'm gonna call it the Fossils."

He wheeze-laughs, his head in Hannah's lap. "You're such an idiot."

"Hey, I gotta get the groaners in while I can. We're dying, dude."

"Now you're just stating the obvious. Hey, where the hell is Gigi? Tesla and Marie are gone, and we're next."

"I'm here."

We whip our heads around (well, as fast as two ancient soon-to-be-cadavers can whip their heads) and see her:

Gigi.

Hannah leaps up – accidentally dropping Pete to the floor, his head bonking the chair leg right next to my face, so now we're both laying on the ground like drunk geezers, it's priceless – and she hugs her, weeping and wailing. "Gigi! Oh my God! You're back! We have to do something! They're dying!"

"Yes. Get them to the doorway."

Hannah cowers. "But.. the flames…"

Gigi hugs her a little tighter. "Trust me."

Then she kneels at my side, picking my head off the carpet.

"Hi Dad."

"Hi honey. So, you did it?"

She smiles. "*We* did it. Yes."

I croak in my tired old-man voice, "Oh, little Gigi. I would say 'I love you,' but it seems so small. What I'm feeling is much bigger than that. Like if love was everything, everywhere, every time, inside everything."

"It is, Dad." she reaches out. "Now take my hand."

I look down at my withering hand, struggling to lift it. "It's… so old… it's almost time, Gigi." I rest my eyes, oh God my eyelids are so heavy, and let out a deep breath, knowing that this is my last breath, jeez, I guess one of them has to be the last, but hey, you know what? I done good. I can live with that. Or I guess die with that.

She jostles my shoulder. "Dad. Open your eyes, you big faker. We've got one last thing to do."

"Ugh. Please. I'm liking this moment. It's a good ending. This is how I want it to end. Like maximum melodrama."

"It's not over, Dad."

"Ugh. I hate saving the multiverse. It's such a pain in the ass."

"You're a pain in the ass."

"Hey, young lady. What did I tell you about cursing?"

"Back in the Boboverse, you actually said everything was bullshit, and I could say whatever the hell I want."

"I don't even remember saying that. I said that?"

"Yes."

"Man, you remember everything."

And so she takes my hands, and Hannah takes Pete's hands, and our two sweet daughters literally drag us across the floor, like mobsters getting rid of dead bodies. I manage to turn my head and wheeze to Pete, "Now *that's* service."

He doesn't even have the strength to laugh or call me an idiot, he just shakes his head, and that's enough. Even the shaking of my best friend's head at one of my lame-ass jokes is a good enough way to go out. Thanks, Pete.

The girls haul our carcasses across the orange, flamey doorway – which is strangely not burning us now – and plop us unceremoniously in the hallway.

"Gigi. Hurry. I think my pancreas just exploded."

"Shush, Dad. I'm working here."

But she's not working, not from where I stand. (Or, more accurately, from where my shriveled up old corpse lays.) She's just crouched down, waiting.

"What are you waiting for, Gigi?"

"God, shut UP, Dad!"

Whoops. Don't want to piss off our only chance of getting out of this alive. I go to zip my lips with my fingers, but my arthritic hands can only get as far as my chin, so I just mutter, "fuck it," and Pete's arthritic hands have just enough energy to reach across and slap me. I deserve it.

And then, finally, after several more of my internal organs expire, the orange subsides, leaving the same old way-too-gray hallway. And in one swift motion, Gigi dials in zero-zero-zero-zero one last time, pulls the door open with the familiar whoosh, and drags us – banging our heads on the *bottom* for the first time, instead of the top – into what I sincerely hope and pray is the year 2020, because if it's not, I turned my body into a pile of ash for absolutely nothing.

I look up at Gigi, who looks younger now, but I can't really tell, because my heart just gave out.

Yup. I'm dead.

20. HOME

From: Chip Collins
To: Everyone
Date: February 29, 2020 8:19pm
Subject: Home.

"What. The. Actual. Fuck?"

It's Fred's voice. I can hear Fred's voice.

If I'm dead, that means Fred is the guy who greets you in heaven. I mean, stranger shit could happen, but *Fred?*

I open one eye.

Fred's standing over me, wagging his finger like a pissed-off middle school chemistry teacher.

"Get up. Now."

Okay, I'm not dead. Check.

I bring my fingers to my eyes and wiggle them around. No wrinkles, no arthritis. Check.

I sit up. And don't puke, for once. Check.

"Look, mister. You're in big trouble."

I look up at him, wanting to say, "Do you have any idea how much trouble we just got you the fuck OUT OF?" but I still don't have the energy. I climb to my feet, awkwardly, these thirty-something-year-old legs are going to need some getting used to. "Fred. What year is it?"

His face goes white. "Oh Christ. How bad was it?"

"Um…"

"Don't even tell me. Just tell me what the hell *that* is."

He turns me around a full one-eighty, so I'm facing the StarCloset. Its door is open, but the door behind it, the INTERDIMENSIONAL TRANSFER APPARATUS…

Is gone.

Gone.

Like it never existed.
Just a wall.

I don't know why, but the only thing I can manage to say is, "Nikola's dead."

And Pete finds my shoulders and puts his arms around me, and we both cry, like the ugliest crying you've ever seen, for our dear, dear, lost friend. Fred, for once at a loss for words or a reprimand, joins us.

After a long time of this, one of the Shrug Team takes my hand and shakes it. "It was an honor, sir." And he peels off his clean suit, and the rest of them follow his lead, and they walk out, and we all know without a shadow of a doubt that the show's over.

The ITA, and Nikola Tesla – in a way they were one and the same, weren't they? – are gone.

• • •

A little hand tugs at my pants leg.

Gigi!

"Go see Old Man! Go see Old Man!"

I pull her up and hug her tight. "No, honey, we can't see Old Man. He's… he's…" and I bury my face in her neck and cry my eyes out all over again.

Thank God she's back. My little Gigi is little again. Thank God. Everything's back to normal. But she won't remember any of this, will she? She doesn't even remember that the Old Man is gone.

Fred pats me on the back. "Um, we'll debrief in a couple of days, how does that sound? You take your time to process. I'll handle the muckety-mucks up top."

So we leave Room 3327 of the New Yorker Hotel, for the last time, ever, I guess, unless I have to rent this room when I'm in the doghouse with Julie, although I'm probably in there pretty good right now, aren't I? I should probably just stop at the registration desk on my way out and book it permanently. They can rename it the Chip Collins Doghouse Room.

By the time the Uber lets us out in front of our apartment, I'm fucking exhausted, like can you imagine what it feels like to go from thirty-four years old to a hundred-and-four and then back again, watch your father figure die right in front of your eyes, say goodbye to your furry alien buddy, and just barely escape The Void? Yeah, that kind of exhausted.

We hump our tired butts up to the second floor, and I immediately plop onto the couch, where I intend to stay for the next three thousand hours (at least), and Pete joins me.

"Holy shit, Pete. Did that just happen?"

"It just happened."

"You want a beer? I can get Gigi to get us a beer."

But he knows I'm kidding, and he gets up, complaining about his lower back, and gets us both a cold one.

I pop it open and we clink, silently toasting Nikola, and forever, and the wordless mix of infinite things we're feeling.

"Pete, you're right, by the way."

"I'm right about a lot of stuff. But what?"

"They're not going to remember any of this. Anything."

Just then the girls come running out of their bedroom, tears in their eyes, both asking, "Bobo?"

"Shit."

Pete fields the question with admirable firmness. "Girls. Bobo had to go home. Just like we came home. He's got a family too. I think. We'll see him again soon, I promise. He's just going to be away for a while. Say bye-bye to Bobo."

"Bye-bye!" They sing together, and just like that, they're off, back to their secret shenanigans. By tomorrow they'll probably forget Bobo even existed.

Just as I'm about to drift off into exhausted-plus-beer land, I hear the key in the front door, and the murmuring of more than two giddy voices in the hall. Me and Pete look around like burglars, like we did in fact just create the biggest mess literally of all time, but to look around the apartment, it's like nothing happened, it's actually cleaner than it usually is by this time on guy's night in.

The girls come stumbling in, Julie and Meg, and oh great, Gina's still with them, and they're hugging and singing some drunken Justin Timberlake song or something, and all three of them plop on our couch.

"Hey honey." Julie plants an exaggerated wet one on my cheek. "Anything interesting happen tonight?" She hiccups.

"Wow, babe. You guys swallow the mojito factory?"

Gina laughs, and slurs, "Ha! You're funny as… I can't… funny, yeah." Here eyes are all googley, God these guys really tied one on. She tries to focus. "Hey, where's my pal Bobo?"

They look around, with that inebriated *you'll-never-find-your-*

keys-even-if-they're-right-in-front-of-you look. I lean over and give Gina a quick hug. "Hey, Gina. Good to see you. Bobo? He went home. To be with all the other Bobos."

They laugh together, like it's the most hilarious joke they've heard all night. Julie slaps my thigh. "You're funny, honey. Did you know you're funny? Bobo. Going home. Ha! Hey, was Gigi good?"

I smile. "Yeah, babe. You have no idea. She saved all our lives."

She smacks me on the knee. "You're so funny! Meg, isn't he funny tonight? Meg?"

But Meg's on the other side of the couch trying to make out with Pete, right there in front of us, and Pete's gently pushing her away, and within two minutes the three of them are passed out and snoring.

So me and Pete quietly get up and sneak into the bedroom where the other girls are playing, and just sit there on the floor and watch them.

Hannah picks up a Barbie doll and walks it over to Gigi. "Barb get married."

Gigi's got a Superman doll – sorry, Ken – and she bends it over to kiss the other doll. "Let's go Paris!"

Pete pats me on the back. "Well, would you look at that. I'm wrong. Maybe they will remember the good stuff."

Gigi notices us now, and puts down her Superman, and walks over, all serious.

"Daddy."

"Yes, honey bumpkin?"

She looks deep into my eyes and scrunches up her face, and I get a feeling, like she's going to say something a thirty-year-old woman would say, or connect directly to my brain. And I realize that inside this little kid is the power of telepathy, and the power to heal, and the ability to find her way around dimensions without a map. Inside that brain somewhere is the memory of walking on the event horizon of a supermassive black hole at the center of a universe. And driving through Paris on Victory Day in 1945. Talking to a dinosaur. Growing into a woman in a matter of hours.

I wonder if she'll remember any of it.

"What are you thinking, honey? Remembering something?"

She looks at me, really concentrating, oh I can feel it, something big, and then…

"Gigi go poop."

Yeah. That's about right.

Start the book with a fart joke and end it with a poop joke.

I like that.

But before I can put my mental pen down and call it a trilogy, Gigi throws her little arms around my neck and giggles.

"Daddy love Gigi. Gigi love Daddy. Forever."

Wow.

Now *that's* an ending.

This book is dedicated to William Terbo, grand-nephew and last living relative of Nikola Tesla. William died in August of 2018.

I had the great fortune to work with William on the first book in this series, *Where the Hell is Tesla?* I had reached out to him for symbolic permission to use Nikola Tesla's name, but it quickly became more about digging a little deeper into the enigmatic inventor and getting things right. We got to speak and correspond many times over a couple of years. He was a quirky guy, William, but absolutely brilliant, and he didn't mind all the f-bombs from Chip, as long as I didn't mess with Nikola Tesla. In fact, I was struck with how devoted he was to his grand-uncle, to getting the facts straight (as few facts as there are in these novels!), to changing Tesla's dialog to things he'd actually say, not things I wanted him to say, to the pronunciation of his name (for the record, he said "Ni-*KO*-la" was correct, or at least acceptable, instead of "*NI*-ko-la"), to generally honoring the great man that he was. I hope I've done that in these books, and maybe even inspired a little more interest in Nikola Tesla, one of his century's greatest minds, and possibly the greatest inventor of all time.

If you're a real fan of this series, you might remember the many times Tesla bends down and tousles Chip's hair, including the first time they meet in book one. That was taken directly from a conversation I had with William, who recounted in vivid detail the memory of, as a wee lad, meeting his grand-uncle for the first time, the great Nikola Tesla, who bent down and tousled little William's hair with a paternal grin on his face. William told me that little story with such fondness, and it really helped me shape the relationship of Tesla and Chip.

William was an engineer and and inventor in his own right, working at NASA and RCA, and he carried the torch for Nikola Tesla for years as Executive Director of the Tesla Memorial Society. What a great guy.

Thank you and goodbye, William.

YOU'VE FINISHED

Please review this book!

One of the best ways for independent authors and small
publishers to get exposure for their books is to receive as many
honest, thoughtful reviews as possible.

Please take a moment to visit the place you purchased it from and
let the world know what you thought!

Thanks in advance!

ALSO BY ROB DIRCKS

The Wrong Unit

I DON'T KNOW WHAT THE HUMANS ARE SO CRANKY ABOUT. Their enclosures are large, they ingest over a thousand calories per day, and they're allowed to mate. Plus, they have me: an Autonomous Servile Unit, housed in a mobile/bipedal chassis. I do my job well: keep the humans healthy and happy.

"Hey you."

Heyoo. That's my name, I suppose. It's easier for the humans to remember than 413s98-itr8. I guess I've gotten used to it.

———

Rob Dircks, bestselling author of *Where the Hell is Tesla?*, has a "unit" with a problem: how to deliver his package, out in the middle of nowhere, with nothing to guide him. Oh, and with the fate of humanity hanging in the balance. It's a science fiction tale of technology gone haywire, unlikely heroes, and the nature of humanity. (Woah. That last part sounds deep. Don't worry, it's not.)

———

"Rob Dircks manages to bridge the tricky divide between science-fiction and humor so effortlessly that a comparison to Vonnegut is not a hyperbolic stretch." - *Ruth Sinanian, Literature Reviewer*

"★★★★★ The Wrong Unit is the right story for today... it reacquaints us with our human ingenuity and shortcomings, our deepest longings, and, most notably, our great capacity to love."

"★★★★★ FUNNY. HUMAN. A GREAT RIDE! The Wrong Unit is a fun and twist-turning journey that keeps you on the edge of your seat."

"★★★★★ I'm such a fan of this book that I'm going to recommend it for next month's Book Club pick!"

"★★★★★ OUTSTANDING!! With The Wrong Unit, Rob Dircks has established himself with this potentially prophetic view into humanity's future and the consequences of our growing reliability on and appetite for technology."

"★★★★★ The Wrong Unit is such a great ride!! The pace is fast, the dialogue is smart and sarcastic and witty. The sci-fi world created by Dircks is new, imaginative, and so original. No easy feat! I loved the main characters Heyoo and Wah. Laugh out loud funny and sure, I'll admit, I got a little weepy at some spots. Highly recommended!"

ALSO BY ROB DIRCKS

You're Going to Mars!

Living and slaving in Fill City One, you get used to the smell. We call it the Everpresent Stink. But every once in a while, on a spring day with a breeze, it clears away enough to remind us that there is something more out there. Most Fillers' wildest dreams would be just to get past the walls and live in the mainland. But my dream? It's a little bigger.

I'm going to Mars.

Well, I'm only going to Mars if I can find a winning Red Scarab to get on Zach Larson's crazy reality show. And then I'll have to figure out how to escape this hellhole. And then compete on live television for three months. And somehow win a spot on the crew of the very first manned mission to Mars. Oh, and one more slight obstacle? There might be a reason that by 2085 a human still hasn't set foot on the Red Planet. A dangerous reason. A reason worth killing for.

––––––––

In *You're Going to Mars!* Rob Dircks, Audible best-selling author of *Where the Hell Is Tesla?*, creates a near-future filled with family (the good kind and the insufferable kind), pop divas, mobsters, and the world's first trillionaire - and sends them all on a science fiction odyssey / comedy / love story / adventure that will change their world forever.

––––––––

"★★★★★ **Reviewers' Choice Award – it's THAT good.** Captivating, interesting and creative. I could not put it down. I would love to see it filmed!" — *AudioBookReviewer.com*

"★★★★★ **One of my favorites of the year!** This book was a pure joy to listen to. One fist-bump moment after another. I enjoyed every minute of it." — *DabOfDarkness Book Reviews*

"★★★★★ **A remarkable book.** *You're Going to Mars!* was one of the most interesting, entertaining stories I've listened to in quite a while. A fabulously written book with a unique plot, endearing characters, and a richly crafted world, You're Going to Mars is one of those books I just didn't want to put down until I finished it." — *BriansBookBlog.com*

"★★★★★ **Mr. Dircks once again hits a home run!** I have been a fan of Mr. Dircks' works from his premiere release… you cannot go wrong giving this book a listen if you like science fiction and great writing." — *Quella Book Reviews*

"★★★★★ **Fun, Fast-Moving, and Genuinely Funny Sci-Fi.** This audiobook was a blast! A comedic sci-fi take on the Charlie and the Chocolate Factory story with a female protagonist. Even though *Ready Player One* was similarly-themed, this book is about as different as you can get, and in many ways a better book." — *Wynne McLaughlin, Author of* The Bone Feud

"★★★★★ **Hits it out of the park again!** Dircks' unflagging ability to imbue plot-crackling science fiction with a deep vein of humor, heart, and hope reminds me of Ray Bradbury with curses. An incredibly inventive plot of a young woman's journey in a world both similar and very different from ours. Wow, just wow." — *Wendy Mass,* New York Times *bestselling author of* Pi in the Sky *and* The Candymakers

ALSO BY ROB DIRCKS

Listen To The Signal: Short Stories Volume 1

Like episodes of The Twilight Zone or The Outer Limits, the sixteen stories contained in Listen To The Signal, Short Stories Volume 1 ask questions like, "What would happen if an iPhone game was addictive - to everyone?" and "Are we all living inside a simulation? And if so, who's running it?" and "When a pilot has to emergency land in a remote town near Area 51 what does he find?"

Hi, Rob Dircks here. I'm the Audible bestselling author of Where the Hell is Tesla?, and I've been writing and narrating these stories since 2016 on my podcast, Listen To The Signal. But now I've made them available ONLY here in this book. They include: Dakō • Today I Invented Time Travel • End Game • November 8, 2016 • Quick Fix • Horatio Breathed His Last • Purgatory • Out of the Blue • Tick Tick Tick • Rose • Red Parka • Bloop • Their DNA Was No Longer the Same • The Last One • Mister Personality • Christmas in Silver Peak.

"★★★★★ There is no one writing scifi as well as Rob Dircks right now, and this short story collection proves it.

I listened to all of these stories when they originally came out on his podcast, and was blown away every time by the quality of his writing and his mastery of the short story form. He knows the tropes and how to subvert them. He can build a world in a few paragraphs so that you understand it intuitively. He creates characters that are uniquely relatable and gosh darn it, he's funny to boot.

That is when he is not making me tear up. Add to all that the fact that he does a terrific job narrating his own stories and you have a very appealing package.

But now that I have been able to re-listen to all the stories again via this collection, hearing them all together rather than strung out over a series of months, I perceived something I had not noticed before. Something that unites not only these stories but also his novels. Something special that only Rob Dircks can deliver.

It's a sweetness, a love of life and humanity, that shines through all of his characters and all of his imaginary worlds. I feel instantly better when I finish something he has written, I feel uplifted and hopeful. What a wonderful gift Rob has to allow us to see the good in one another, and how lucky we are that he is sharing it with us through his art.

Can't wait for the next collection."

ABOUT THE AUTHOR

Rob Dircks is the Audible bestselling author of *Where the Hell is Tesla?*, *The Wrong Unit*, *Don't Touch the Blue Stuff! (Where the Hell is Tesla? Book Two)*, and a member of SFWA (Science Fiction & Fantasy Writers of America). His prior work includes the anti-self-help book *Unleash the Sloth! 75 Ways to Reach Your Maximum Potential By Doing Less*, and a drawerful of screenplays and short stories. Some of these sci-fi short stories appear on Rob's original audio short story podcast *Listen To The Signal*, also narrated by the author. Rob's a big fan of classic science fiction, and sci-fi conspiracy theories (not to believe in them, just for entertainment.) When not writing, he's helping other authors publish their own work with his own little imprint, Goldfinch Publishing. He lives in New York with his wife and two kids. You can get in touch at www.robdircks.com.

facebook.com/robdircksauthor

twitter.com/RobDircks

instagram.com/Rob.Dircks

goodreads.com/robdircks

amazon.com/author/robdircks

www.ingramcontent.com/pod-product-compliance
Lightning Source LLC
Chambersburg PA
CBHW022025120726
47898CB00007BA/2525